Autumn Career

A novel by Brian Sherwin

Brian Sherwin asserts the moral right to be identified as the author of this work.

All characters and events in this publication, other than those clearly in the public domain, are fictitious, and any resemblance to real persons, living or dead, is purely coincidental.

ISBN 978-1-0369-0633-7

Autumn Career

Chapter 1 - 14th September 2022

Thankfully Boland answered my knock himself. I lifted the pistol from my bag and shot him squarely in the chest. He was thrown backwards into the hallway and didn't even scream. The noise of the shot was explosive and made me feel that the whole street had heard it. I dropped the pistol back into the bag, turned and walked the four metres from the porch to the gate. There was nobody to be seen. I turned right and walked quickly into the dark park. The entire operation had taken about ten seconds.

Once in the park I walked quickly down the footpath leading to the playground. As it was dark and raining the park was empty. After about a hundred metres I turned left, crouched low, and walked quickly across the park towards Donbas Street. If I had been seen entering the park after the shot it would have appeared that I was heading for Curlew Road leading to a main road to the town centre. I reached a garden hedge leading towards Donbas Street and stopped to draw breath. Still no sign of anyone. At seventy-four I was quite fit for my age, but the exertion of the past few minutes had left me short of breath and the shock had left me trembling. I stood for three minutes to recover my breath.

The sound of a police car or ambulance siren approaching made me get moving again. I stepped out onto the footpath and proceeded slowly at a pace suitable to a frail old lady going home with a shopping bag. I had to walk past about forty houses to get to the railway lane. I met just one person, a young man in his twenties who was hurrying and paid me no attention whatsoever. Once on the railway lane, I increased speed as I was again alone and could not be seen. On reaching the metal footbridge I reverted to my slow pained walk and crossed it slowly. I met nobody, made it to the roundabout, and took the road to the town centre.

I was now walking along a busy road and would be seen by many drivers, so I maintained slow walking mode, slightly bent over with the weight of the bag. I was dressed in a dark blue overcoat and a multi-coloured woollen hat. It took about an hour to get to Taunton town centre and from there to the railway station, a boomerang shaped route from the crime scene. I already had my return ticket from Bristol Temple Meads to Taunton. I made my way to platform 2 to wait for the next train to Bristol. The information screen told me that it was due at 19.45 hours which meant a thirty-minute wait. Although it was cold and wet, I sat on an outside bench on the platform rather than in the crowded waiting room. There, I had sandwiches and hot coffee which were part of the contents of the shopping bag. The other contents of the bag were new clothes which I had purchased that afternoon in Taunton. As I stepped onto the train, I dropped the woollen hat into a wastepaper unit beside the carriage door. If found, it would confirm that I had left Taunton for Bristol. At 19.47, the train pulled out of the station and for the first time all day I relaxed. Had I managed to pull it off successfully?

At Temple Meads, I took a bus to the city centre. From there, I took a bus to Fishponds where I recovered my car from a side street. From Bristol to my home in North Devon is 100 miles via the M5 and the A361 (North Devon Link Road). My route home avoiding both main routes added 27 miles to the journey.

In order to avoid Closed Circuit TV cameras (CCTV), I avoided 'A' roads as much as possible and made my way to Bishops Lydeard a few miles from Taunton. From there it was across Exmoor via Wheddon Cross, Exford, and Simonsbath. At Exford, the public toilet in the carpark provided welcome relief although it risked my car being seen and remembered. I also risked parking in the entrance to a forest to take a thirty-minute nap as my eyes were tired. The car was parked in such a way that it could not be seen from the road.

Between Simonsbath and Challacombe I had a puncture in the front offside tyre, my first puncture in years. What bad luck. I had a spare wheel but had never changed a wheel before on this car. I was terrified that if a car came from either direction whilst I was changing the wheel the driver would stop to assist and thus become a witness to my presence on Exmoor that night. I decided to tell any motorist helper that I was returning from visiting my son in Lytham StAnnes near Blackpool.

It took me ages to work out how the jack worked. I even had to lie down and stick my head under the car to see where the jack fitting was and how to connect it. It was pitch dark and I only had a small torch. Eventually, I got the jack working and raised the car. In my panic and hurry I forgot to loosen the nuts before lifting the car and then had to lower it again to loosen them. They were so tight that I had to stand on the spanner and use my weight to loosen them. One nut was stubborn but with perseverance I managed to loosen it. The spare wheel was heavy, and it was a struggle lifting the wheel and fitting it onto the five wheel bolts, but eventually managed it. I was now very dirty, tired, and irritable and the task had taken me over an hour. However, during that time not, a single car had passed from either direction. I marvelled at how remote Exmoor was for this to happen and thanked my lucky stars.

It was nearly 2am when I drove quietly into my village and into the drive of my bungalow. I parked the car where it could be seen by passers-by on the road. The pistol was put in its place under the loose floorboard in my bedroom and I had a bath and went to bed exhausted. I had a good night's sleep.

Chapter 2

Jane Boland was having a bath when she heard the shot downstairs. She dried herself quickly, put on a dressing gown and rushed downstairs. Nigel was lying in a pool of blood and appeared lifeless. She knelt down, touched his face and called his name but got no response. Jane realised that Nigel was dead. The front door was open, so she ran to the gate. No sign of anybody. Back inside she dialled 999, asked for ambulance and police, quickly explained to both emergency services what had happened and gave her address. The first police car arrived in seven minutes.

During the next few hours, the police carried out door to door calls around Boland's neighbourhood in a search for witnesses, but no one had seen anything suspicious. No car or motorcycle or bicycle had been seen moving on any of the surrounding roads before or after the shooting. A check on local buses and taxis turned up nothing and CCTV at Taunton Railway Station and Bus Station showed nobody who looked suspicious that evening. CCTV on the main roads leading towards the crime scene produced a short list of vehicles which had been close to the scene before the incident and left within an hour but each of these were checked and ruled out.

During the investigation the police felt that this killing had all the hallmarks of a professional gangland killing or possibly a family feud. Boland was well known to them as a drug dealer and receiver of stolen property. He had convictions on both fronts and had served a two-year prison sentence as a young man.

The bullet was from a Browning 9mm, and the markings were not from a known gun.

Many of Boland's acquaintances were questioned and most of the known Taunton drug dealers and users but the police remained baffled. They also checked with all their local contacts to see if there were any rumours about who did the killing. There were rumours but none to give the police any real leads.

Boland's murder was extensively covered in the local Somerset County Gazette and had just brief mentions in the national papers.

Over the next few weeks, the Gazette covered the police search for the killer, but it became evident that there were no real leads or suspects. However, there was always the possibility that the police knew much more about the killing than they were letting on.

A wave of fear spread across Taunton and the surrounding area particularly within the criminal fraternity. More rumours began circulating about the likely killer and people became cautious about answering knocks on their door particularly after dark.

But after a month or so the killing faded from the news and from local gossip and Taunton settled back to normal.

Chapter 3

Nigel Boland was fifty-five when he died. Born in London in 1967 he lived in Brentford until aged twenty. As a teenager he became involved with local gangs and gradually drifted into a life of crime. At first it was burglaries for which he served a one-year sentence when aged twenty. He then progressed to drug dealing and was employed by a major London dealer for four years. This came to an abrupt halt when aged twenty-six he was caught in a drugs raid by the police and was sentenced to four years in prison, whilst his drug baron boss managed to escape prison as all the evidence pointed to Boland. He learnt some important lessons from this experience. The secret of success lay in ensuring that the people who worked for you took the rap if things went wrong. On his release from prison, he made a decision to move to a provincial town and set up a drug dealing business on his own.

He moved to Taunton where he rented a flat, found a number of suitable characters to work for him and using his contacts in London to supply him, set up a drugs dealership. He supplied cannabis, cocaine, amphetamines and heroin. All deliveries were to his employees and all dealing was carried out by them. His dealers were not allowed to have any drugs on them when they visited Boland, and no drugs were ever kept in his flat.

The business grew rapidly and within a few years he had a team of ten working for him. Needless to say, there was no payroll. No Income Tax or National Insurance was paid, and no books were kept identifying these as employees. All business was conducted in cash. He became the largest drug supplier in Somerset County. Once or twice a year one of his dealers was caught by the police and sent to prison for periods varying from one to three years. Boland created a 'sick pay' scheme for his staff whereby their families were paid the national minimum living wage of over £400 per week whilst they were inside. His team considered this to be very generous, overlooking the fact that they took all the risks while he took most of the profits.

The police in Taunton were well aware of Boland's activities and were very keen to take him down but he was continually successful at ensuring that there was never direct evidence leading to him.

Boland met his future wife at a party in Taunton when he was 32 and she was 25. Jane knew from the outset about Nigel's life of crime and although she was not comfortable with his career choice she liked the lifestyle he could provide her, so she accepted what he was and supported him through thick and thin.

Nigel and Jane had a son Martin born in 1999. When aged 19 he joined his father's business as head of security and quickly developed a tough guy reputation.

Over his 24 years as the main drug dealer in Taunton Nigel Boland's position had been challenged a few times. He knew that he had to demonstrate his authority with a show of strength on these occasions and gained a reputation for ruthlessness. One contender disappeared and several days later was found in the river Tone having died from strangulation. The killer was never identified. Another was found dead in his home from an overdose of heroin. His family and acquaintances were adamant that he was not a heroin user. It was never established who had administered the fatal injections. A third competitor had a near fatal car accident when a front wheel fell off at high speed. Four of the wheel nuts were missing and one was loose and had sheared off.

Boland felt that he was invincible and took a casual approach to his own security. His house was alarmed to detect any intruders, he had a driver for his car which was garaged miles from his home and he had a Rottweiler dog in the house. There were security cameras around the external areas of the house which were monitored by screens on his son's phone. Apart from that he depended on his own quick reactions and self-defence skills to repel any attacker.

On the evening he was shot, the Rottweiler was out in the rear garden, and the sight of an elderly woman at his front door as seen on the monitor did not alert Boland to any danger.

Chapter 4 September 2022

My name is Lorna Cooper. I am seventy-four years old and I am fit and healthy. Born in Somerset I have spent most of my life in England apart from a few postings abroad during my husband's military career.

I had a happy childhood and a good education and qualified as a dental technician at the age of twenty-two. I met my future husband when aged thirty-two, got married and had two children. I gave up my dental job when my second child was born and concentrated from then on with domestic activities. I was perfectly happy with my lot until I reached my seventies when I realised that I had led a rather mundane existence and made no major mark on the world.

I became a widow four years ago. My husband John had a long and distinguished army career followed by twenty happy years of retirement in North Devon. To be more accurate it was semi-retirement as John became a security advisor after leaving the army and worked with a local firm advising and installing home security systems. He retired from this aged sixty-seven and then at the age of seventy-one developed lung cancer and after 6 difficult months illness died in our local hospital. And yes, he had been a smoker for over fifty years.

Following John's death, I was broken-hearted and became a bit of a recluse. I had a good friendly relationship with my near neighbours, but this did not go beyond chatting whenever we met and after Church on Sundays. The postman Arthur is a very friendly man and always finds time to stop and chat for a few minutes when he delivers to me. Although I do not get many letters, I have an arrangement with Arthur that he delivers the 'Telegraph' to me six days a week. He delivers between 8.30 and 9.00 every morning so I am often still in bed when he comes, but if I am up and dressed we always chat for a few minutes.

I also have a friend who was a colleague of John's in the army. His name is Tom Rouse and he lives just 12 miles from my home. Tom is a widower having lost his wife two years ago, also following cancer. After his wife's death Tom and I continued our friendship and regularly have meals out and occasionally go to the theatre together. We cook meals for one another every few weeks and sometimes go for walks on Exmoor and along the coast. I enjoy his company and our friendship is purely platonic which suits us both.

Getting used to my own company took quite a while. Although over seventy I felt that I had some useful life left and gradually became convinced that I should do something positive for my remaining few years.

John and I had two children who had kept me busy for many years. During our marriage I tended to live in John's shadow and to applaud his many achievements in the army and devoted my time and energies to looking after the home and children.

John had left to me all his worldly belongings which included a three-bedroom bungalow on a half-acre of land on the edge of a beautiful village called Rishlew near Barnstaple in Devon, a two-year-old BMW 2 Series Gran Coupe, a vintage Jaguar Car (1990), an army Widows Pension and investments worth over £100,000. Among his personal belongings were a pistol and a rifle which he had somehow acquired and took home whilst in the army. There was also a substantial quantity of ammunition for both guns. These had always been kept hidden underneath a loose length of floorboard in the main bedroom and even the children were never told or knew of their existence.

With a mortgage-free house, an army pension, an old age state pension and some investment income I was reasonably well-off especially as I lived a quiet life with no expensive habits, so I did not need to work and was probably too old to get a job anyway.

My two children both live a considerable distance from me. Anne who is forty-one this year has lived in Perth in Western Australia for fourteen years and is married with 2 children. John and I visited them every two years and I visited them alone last year for a wonderful month. As Anne and Rob are farmers, they find it difficult to leave the farm but they came to stay with me for two weeks after John died.

Simon is aged forty and lives in Lytham StAnnes which is just outside Blackpool. He is also married and has a daughter aged eight. Since John died, I have visited them for a few days twice each year, and they visit me twice a year and usually stay for four or five days.

Anne, has a degree in Agriculture and Simon is a Commercial Solicitor. I feel lucky and proud to have reared two children successfully and to see them have good careers and happy relationships and lovely children.

My life since John died has been quiet and non-eventful. I have aways enjoyed my own company and seldom feel lonely. My friendship with Tom fulfils my need for socialising. I have a large garden which is divided into a vegetable garden and a lawn and flower garden. Eight years ago, John and I converted the vegetable section into six raised garden beds, each standing a metre high and filled with good topsoil. I grow a variety of vegetables each year and the raised beds makes it easy work without the need for bending or kneeling. The flower garden comprises beds surrounding a lawn both of which are easy to manage.

I like to walk and as I live close to Exmoor and on the North Devon coast there are many beautiful walks within a few miles from my home. My walks are often with Tom.

I read the Daily Telegraph every day and take the Sunday Times and Sunday Telegraph every Sunday. This keeps me up to date with what is happening in the country and the world and maintains my keen interest in politics. I also read books and have a particular interest in biographies of famous leaders both historical and current.

I enjoy cooking and have maintained the habit of cooking proper meals every day even though it is usually only for myself.

I am a regular attendee at my local Church of England church although I would not describe myself as a religious person.

I attend a number of village events throughout the year and am known to everyone in the village. I would say that I have no enemies, but also that I have no close friends other than Tom. The other close friends I had in the past have each died, and I have not been minded to cultivating new ones.

I watch selected programmes on TV as well as the evening news.

My computer skills are limited but I have a laptop and an iPhone and use emails, online banking, word and excel, and make and receive facetime calls with my children and grandchildren in Australia and Lancashire. I use google to research items of interest and occasionally listen to podcasts in bed.

A quiet and unremarkable existence with which I was reasonably content but somehow left me feeling unfulfilled and inadequate.

This feeling changed after my adventure in Taunton. I felt useful and excited again.

A friend Sylvia who lived in Taunton died last year from a broken heart. Her only grandson had died a year previously at the age of nineteen from a heroin overdose. Sylvia was devastated by this and following his death her health had failed rapidly. She died from a heart attack, but I was sure that it was her grandson's death that led to her death.

It was after reading a story in the Sunday Times about the drugs problems in the South-West of England and learning that the obnoxious trade in Taunton was controlled and managed by a gangland boss named Boland, that I got the idea of avenging my friend and her grandson's deaths by killing Nigel Boland.

I was able to establish his address in Taunton from the Electoral Roll. I read that his home had been raided by police a number of times but on each occasion, they failed to gather sufficient evidence to convict him. It was well known in the Taunton area that he was a dealer and that he employed a number of minor dealers who handled, stored and distributed the merchandise. Knowing that he was damaging the lives of many gave me the idea of taking him out and setting an example and warning to other dealers throughout the country.

I have felt for many years that the law was too soft on drug smugglers and dealers. After what happened to my friend's grandson, I had heard of many other horrific cases of the effect that drugs had on the mental and physical welfare of addicts and the anguish and distress this caused to the families and friends of these unfortunate people.

Chapter 5

Now that I have taken the momentous step of removing Boland, how do I feel! Well, I feel good. The killing of a drug dealer had briefly made national news on TV, Radio and the Newspapers. The general consensus was that this was rough justice, and that society did not regret his loss. It should serve as a reminder to people in the illegal drugs business that punishment can come out of the blue.

I also feel rather pleased that I had managed to achieve the killing successfully and without being caught. By all accounts the police do not know who committed the crime and seem to believe that it was probably a rival killing.

What I had done was clearly a serious crime and I would spend the remainder of my days in prison if caught. I had made the decision that it was worth the risk and if caught I would take my punishment stoically.

My daughter and son would be shocked, horrified and embarrassed to learn what their mother had done but I could only hope that they would understand my motive and eventually might even accept it and forgive me. They were getting on with their lives and leaving me to get on with what remained of mine so I must do what I must do.

I began to consider killing again but realised that I would have to become much more organised at covering my tracks and leaving no trail of evidence to lead the police to me. I also needed to learn some new skills in order to become more professional if I was to kill another enemy of society.

I had managed to kill Boland with one shot because it was at very close range. But there was also an element of luck as a shot in the chest does not always kill and if his reaction to me had been faster it could have gone disastrously wrong.

I needed to learn to shoot the pistol properly and accurately and to be prepared to fire multiple shots quickly if necessary. I also needed to learn how to maintain the gun to ensure its reliability and accuracy.

Regarding covering my tracks, I needed to consider many things to conceal my identity, and to ensure that even if identified there would be no evidence to link me to the crimes. In addition to avoiding cameras on the way home from Bristol I had taken the precaution of leaving my mobile phone at home that day.

I would need to disguise myself for any future mission and decided on a blond wig, a pair of glasses with prominent frames, and clothing which was different from my normal attire. The application of some make-up, which I do not normally use, would also help to alter my appearance.

Chapter 6 - 9th November 2022

Today I set off on a reconnaissance mission. The next potential target lives in Cheltenham. Setting out at 8am I drove to Bristol using the North Devon Link Road, and the M5. I left the motorway at Gordano Services and drove into Bristol via the Suspension Bridge and then left the car on a quiet street about a mile from the city centre. I took a taxi from there to the railway station at Bristol Parkway, a journey of eight miles using the M32. From here I got a return rail ticket to Cheltenham.

The previous week I had travelled to London on a daytrip to do some shopping. I purchased a long ash-blond wig, a pair of glasses with dark red frames, a Camel pure wool double-breasted coat with pockets, and a variety of make-up, all of which I was wearing as I got the taxi in Bristol. The make-up was eyeshadow, mascara, and red lipstick.

Arrived at Cheltenham at 12.30pm and took a bus to the town centre. I made my way to the library. I knew the name of my target but not his address. A search through the electoral registers for each Cheltenham constituency established his address as being near the racecourse, and also indicated that only he and his wife lived at the house. A short bus ride took me close to the address and I set off walking. As anticipated the address led me to a very expensive looking house set in its own grounds. Set in about two acres it had a 100 metres drive from the road to the house. No security on the gate which was open but there were probably cameras closer to the house to warn of intruders. There was a Mercedes Sports parked outside the house.

I could see a road to the left a short distance away, so I set off to explore the lay of the land at the back of the house. The road to the left led into a modern housing estate. A few hundred metres down this road there was a lane leading to the garages and rear garden gates of houses both left and right. I walked along this lane and was pleased to easily identify the back of the target house. The rear garden was bordered at the sides and the back with an eight-foot-high fence. There was a strong metal gate set into the fence to provide a rear exit. This was secured on the inside with a combination padlock securing a bolt lock. A window cutout in the gate allowed for a hand to be put in to manipulate the combination padlock. I reached in and tugged the padlock and to my surprise it sprung open – the last person to lock the gate had failed to spin the combination numbers, a common mistake. I took the open padlock off the bolt, opened the bolt and the gate opened. Without going in I locked the gate again and secured the combination lock and spun the numbers. The combination code was 92175 which I memorised before spinning the numbers. I continued along the lane for a hundred metres or so and then stopped to write the code on the back of my hand. The lane continued for another three hundred metres with the rear gardens of houses on both left and right and then ended with a fence and hedge leading into a field.

The last house on the right-hand side (opposite side to the target house) had an unlocked gate and I could see that the side of the house was unobstructed leading to the front of the house. I decided to enter this property and see if I could get to the front gate unchallenged. If challenged I would beg forgiveness and say that I was too tired to go back the way I had come. As it turned out I was able to walk on a footpath through the rear garden, round the side of the house and along the front footpath to the gate which was open. No sign of life. From there it was a short walk to the main road where I was able to get a bus to the city centre. By now it was 4.40pm and I was hungry. I had a Spaghetti Milanese and coffee in an Italian restaurant and then took a taxi to the station in time to catch a 6pm train to Bristol Parkway. During this journey of less than an hour I wrote notes on the layout of the target house and the combination number. From Bristol Parkway station I took a taxi to where my car was parked. Once back in the car I stopped at a service area, where I removed the wig, glasses, camel coat and make-up. On the drive home there was no need to worry about CCTV cameras, so I took the M5 and the A361 Link Road. Home safe by 9.30pm

A long day out but some very important knowledge gained.

Autumn Career

Chapter 7 - 14th November 2022

If my vigilante activity was to continue without making mistakes or getting caught, I needed to improve my skill with the pistol. Although I had known how to shoot the pistol successfully at close range I had no real experience of handling, aiming and shooting it.

The pistol is a Browning 9mm (Hi-Power). This was the pistol used by the British Army for over 40 years up to 2013. It weighs a kilo and is just under 20 centimetres long. It is a semi-automatic but must be cocked (hammer pulled back) before the first round can be fired. It is loaded with 13 rounds of 9 by 19mm bullets and has an effective firing range of 50 metres. That's the technical description. For the non-technical it is quite heavy, should only be cocked just before firing and has a strong recoil when fired.

My home is just ten miles from Exmoor which is a magnificent National Park covering two hundred and sixty-seven square miles with moorland, woods and coastal areas. When John was living, we regularly explored Exmoor with drives and long walks. There are off-road areas where you can walk for miles without seeing anyone.

I decided that a remote valley near the Devon/Somerset border would become my secret shooting range.

Although I could probably avoid being seen personally, my car would be seen as I would have to park it to go walking. I would use the old Jaguar for such trips. This was parked in a lock-up garage on a farm adjoining my village and it needed to be driven regularly to keep it in good condition. It was registered in my name, and I kept it taxed and insured.

I cleaned and oiled the pistol, using instructions downloaded from the internet (using a library computer), prepared a picnic lunch and dressed in hiking boots, waterproof leggings a heavy waterproof oiled jacket and hat, and set off for Exmoor. My backpack had everything I would need including a hundred rounds of bullets, a pair of ear defenders, binoculars, an unregistered burner phone which I had bought in Tesco for £20, a camera, and some target sheets (printed from the internet). Lastly, I packed some spare dry clothes.

It was a cold and downcast day in mid-November and there was very little traffic on Exmoor. I parked in a visitor's carpark and set off overland for my quiet valley. Walking through gorse and heather can be quite hard work and it took over an hour to reach my destination, which was at the bottom of a deep valley surrounded by hills. I rested for twenty minutes and surveyed the landscape carefully with the binoculars. There was nobody to be seen. At 10.30 am I set up four target sheets on a stone outcrop about 15 metres from where I sat. I would be shooting into a hill so there was no danger of hitting any person or animal behind the targets.

Having studied videos on YouTube (at Exeter Library) I knew how to hold, cock, aim and shoot the Browning. It took a while to get used to shooting the semi-automatic and it was not until the 16th shot that I managed to hit the target. By slowing down and taking careful steady aim, with my arm outstretched I began to hit the target most times.

Even with the ear defenders the noise was deafening. I felt sure that the shots could be heard for miles and that it would not be long before a park warden, a farmer, or even a walker would come to investigate. After firing about 50 shots I took down the targets, put away the pistol and settled down to a most enjoyable lunch. I allowed an hour to pass keeping a close watch on the surrounding landscape and nobody appeared.

During my lunch a group of nine Red Deer Hinds came down the valley and it was not until they were about 50 metres away from me that they spotted me. They stopped and remained still just watching me for about 5 minutes. I enjoyed this very much and was not in any way scared as I knew that Red Deer do not attack humans. The exception to this is during the rutting season in October when Stags may attack a human who ventures too near them. The Hinds were beautiful looking with sleek brown coats, and I marvelled that such large wild animals still wandered freely in crowded England and were so elusive that they were seldom seen. An honour indeed. Eventually I stood up and they immediately turned and took off at a gallop. They climbed a hill effortlessly and disappeared over the skyline. Their visit worried me however because after all the shooting an hour earlier it was unlikely that these deer would make their way down this particular valley. It must have meant that they had to come down the valley to get away from a person or persons further up the valley. I decided not to risk continuing my target practice without first establishing if there was a person in the valley. I packed up all my things leaving no trace of having been there and made my way back through the valley towards my car.

I met a couple of walkers as I neared the carpark and stopped to exchange pleasantries with them. They were a couple from Chelmsford on a walking holiday. They admitted that they did not like to venture too far off the road, so I felt reassured that they had been nowhere near to me earlier in the day. We walked back to the carpark together and they set off back to Combe Martin, a seaside resort where they were staying. After twenty minutes I felt that it was safe to return to where I had been in the morning and resume shooting practice.

The second session went very well with a 90% success rate. It was surprising how quickly my aim improved and it became clear that with practice I could become a competent marksman. I set off for home confident that I could use the gun properly and hit a target from twenty-five metres or less nine times out of ten.

I recovered my car and had a pleasant drive home. The Jaguar was a pleasure to drive and, as always, I felt pleased that I had kept the car despite the expense.

Chapter 8 - 24th November 2022

My target in Cheltenham was a wealthy businessman who was a major supporter and contributor to "Just Stop Oil", a group of 'green' activists who wanted the government to speed up the programme of reducing carbon emissions, transitioning to clean renewable energy, and in particular to stop the issue of further licences for North Sea Oil exploration. His name was Ernest Matthews, and he had very publicly contributed a million pounds to the "Just Stop Oil" group.

Their campaign of disrupting the public by blocking roads and motorways was a disgrace and it was infuriating that the police allowed them to disrupt society at will. People were prevented from getting to work, to hospitals, to funerals, weddings and many other important activities. These misguided protestors were happy to break the law, cared little for the pain and inconvenience they inflicted on society, and ironically were doing more harm than good to their 'green' cause than they could imagine in their stupidity. They were seen by the majority of people as nasty, ignorant fools who contributed nothing to society and had no social conscience despite their so-called noble motives.

It would be good to send a warning that there can be a big price to pay for their actions.

Having established the lay of the land earlier I set off for Cheltenham on a Friday late in November. Avoided the

Link Road and the Motorway and parked in the suburbs at 4.30 pm and made my way via two bus trips to the target area. I was dressed in dark trousers and waterproof shoes and a black overcoat. I had black gloves and a black scarf in my coat pocket and a pair of glasses with a dark red frame. I carried a large handbag which held the gun as well as a few personal items. I had no telephone or bank cards with just cash in my purse.

At 5.30 I arrived outside the house and found the gate closed and locked. I wandered up and down the road on alternate sides for forty minutes, when a car arrived at the house gate and the gate opened automatically. The driver clearly had a remote device to open the gate. The car drove in, and the gate remained open as it drove up to the house. I walked towards the property and slipped in the gate and turned right onto the lawn. About 10 seconds after entering the gate it closed, again automatically, either on a time lapse or having been remotely signalled to close from the house.

I hurried to a shrub and hid behind it. Here I arranged the scarf over my head and neck so that only my eyes were visible and put on the gloves and glasses. I then made my way quickly along the fence past the side of the house and to the back gate. While sheltering the combination lock inside my open overcoat and using a pencil torch I set the combination at 92175 and tested it. I then relocked the gate and lock but left the combination on the release number to ensure that I could make a fast getaway. Then I put the loaded pistol in my coat pocket together with a pork pie and bottle of water and left my handbag on the grass in the corner nearest the gate.

This all took a few minutes, and I then remained very still for about ten minutes to see if any alarm had been raised. All was quiet. Clearly if there was a CCTV camera monitoring the front gate it had not been looked at in the last 15 minutes.

I retraced my footsteps to the side of the house staying close to the fence. I stopped where I had a view of any activity outside either the front or rear of the house. It was a fairly mild evening with a dark cloudy sky. From time to time the clouds cleared and the moon lit up the garden which was mainly lawn, interspersed with shrubs and trees. When this occurred, I kept well hidden behind a shrub.

After a couple of hours, the back door was opened, and a man came out. He triggered a security light which lit up the back clearly. I could see that the man was Ernest Matthews, my target. He stood a few metres from the back door and lit up a cigarette. I hoped that this was a nightly routine. From where I stood, he would see me if I crossed the lawn towards him. I calculated that if I had been standing at the side of the house near the corner, I would not have been seen by him and could step out from the corner to within 2 metres of him.

Would he come out for another smoke later in the evening! Fairly likely as he probably did not smoke in the house.

It was now 8.10pm and it was likely that this was an after-dinner smoke. He might have another before going to bed. I decided to wait until 11pm. If he failed to re-appear I would abort the mission and try again in a week's time.

Up until 10 pm I kept walking slowly up and down the garden keeping close to the fence. From 10pm onwards I stood at the side of the house close to the rear corner with my hand on the pistol.

At 10.40 I heard the back door open, and the security light came on. I crept to the corner and risked peering around the back. I cocked the gun and stepped out towards him. He did not hear me, and I reached his side unnoticed. I raised the pistol and shot him just above the ear. He spurted blood as he fell, and I knew that he was dead.

I immediately hurried over to the fence and headed for the back gate. I collected my handbag, and the combination lock opened as soon as I pulled it. From the moment of the shot, it took about one minute to clear the property, re-lock the gate and spin the combination wheels. With the pistol in my handbag, I walked quickly along the lane until I reached the fence at its end.

All looked quiet at the end house on the right. I realised by then that I had been splashed with blood on my face and coat. Using what remained in the water bottle and a handkerchief I cleaned my face and coat as best I could. I then entered the rear gate of the end house and made for the side of the house. Halfway up the garden path a dog started barking. I cocked the pistol ready to deal with it but as I neared the house, I could see the dog held by a chain outside his kennel. I put away the gun and ran until I reached the front gate which was bolted but unlocked. Once outside I turned left and walked like an old lady to the main road. I did not dare to look back in case I was being watched. Rather than wait at the bus-stop visible from the house I had just left I continued walking to the next stop. After 15 minutes a bus for the city arrived and I got it. The scarf was now arranged to cover the front of my coat, and I hoped that my face was clear of blood. Ten minutes later I alighted in the city centre.

I took another bus to the suburb where the car was parked and reached it by 11.45pm. As far as I could tell no-one had paid me any attention on either bus or whilst I was in the city centre. It was a huge relief to sit into the car. My head was spinning, and I was shaking, and I felt totally drained.

After a few minutes I set off on the same route home as I had come, avoiding the M5, the North Devon Link Road and all major towns.

Much of modern technology had passed me by. I knew that the police used all sorts of modern techniques to solve crimes including drones, DNA, location tracking from telephone data, numberplate recognition and many other techniques which I was only vaguely aware of. I would take what precautions I could to avoid being detected but I must be prepared for being identified and caught at any time. My days of freedom were numbered.

On the long journey home, I considered what I had done. The man I had killed had not actually committed any crime. He probably firmly believed in the danger to the planet created by carbon emissions and felt that he should do something to help encourage the government to speed up progress towards using clean energy and eliminating the use of oil. By giving a million pounds to the 'Just Stop Oil' campaign it did not necessarily mean that he condoned their illegal disruptive actions. Perhaps it had been unfair of me to choose him.

But then I considered his actions in another way. He would have known about all the disruptive activities and that his money would be used to facilitate more, so by facilitating the disruptive activities he was effectively a participant. It might even be considered that facilitating the disruptive activities but not taking part in them was more anti-social than being a participant.

What would normally take about 3 to 4 hours took 5 hours which included a half-hour nap on Exmoor. I climbed into bed at 5am and went into a deep sleep.

Chapter 9

Ernest Matthews was 62 when he died. Born and educated in Manchester he declined the opportunity to go to university and instead started his career as a trader. Initially he traded in vegetables. With his father's help he purchased a van and started buying vegetables and fruit from farmers and selling them to independent grocers and fruit and veg shops. This was successful and he soon had three vans on the road with two employees. After a few years he expanded his business by trading in fresh fish. With a refrigerated van he would drive to Billingsgate in London, purchase a van load of fresh fish, return to Manchester and supply fish to independent shops and to some small groups of shops. This gradually expanded to also selling fish to hotels and restaurants. By the age of twenty-seven he was the main wholesale supplier of fruit, vegetables and fish in the Manchester area. He then started to expand his trading area and became a major supplier across the midlands including Liverpool, Blackpool, Leeds, Bradford and Sheffield.

Gradually he became a millionaire and then a multi-millionaire and at the age of sixty sold his business and retired.

He married Marie when he was thirty and they had three children who had established successful careers. He and Marie led an active social life and attended many functions and events together.

Matthews had always been interested in politics and had time to indulge his interest once retired. He believed passionately in the dangers of global warming, and it was this passion that led him to support 'Just Stop Oil', a group of protesters who developed a campaign of protest which involved disrupting society in the United Kingdom. They blocked bridges, railways roads and motorways for lengthy periods causing massive disruption to the economy and to society. They believed that the publicity they got from these major public disruptions would force the government to take faster action to move the country to cleaner green energy and away from using fossil fuels which were causing global warming. They considered that their campaign had already been partially successful as the government had recently announced that ‘fracking’ would be banned.

Fracking was a method of extracting natural gas from underground rocks by fracturing them to allow gas to flow from the cracks. This had been very successful in the USA, making them self-sufficient in natural gas. Protesters claimed that disruptions would bring their demands to the forefront in the media. They maintained that in addition to being a fossil fuel, fracking could cause earthquakes. There was little evidence to support this, and the USA did not have any earthquake problems despite their intensive fracking. Banning fracking was a major mistake by the government as it meant that the country could not move towards self-sufficiency in gas and would have to continue to import gas from countries who cared little about 'saving the planet'.

By funding 'Just stop Oil' Matthews enabled them to maintain their campaign by paying their travel and accommodation costs and paying their fines when prosecuted.

He was aware that their activities were unpopular with those affected but felt that any pain they were inflicting on the public was necessary to force the government to act on their demands.

Matthews was also a supporter of several worthy charities. It was established after his death that he had donated over £3 million to various charities over a period of ten years. He was admired and liked by his family, friends and community. His funeral was attended by hundreds of people and his published obituaries all pointed to him having been a good man.

Chapter 10 - 25th November 2022

At around mid-day I awoke feeling very panicky. Had I been seen by anyone? Had I been picked up by CCTV? Had the neighbours heard me arrive home? The gun was still in my handbag and my coat had blood on it. How could I be so careless? Clearly some covering-up actions needed to be taken. It was no longer safe to keep the pistol (and the rifle) in the house. I decided to list out the preventative precautions I needed to consider.

The Pistol and Rifle: For years these had been stored under a loose section of floorboard in the main bedroom. They now had to leave the house. In the short term, I would wrap them both in towels and waterproof cellophane and store them in the lock-up garage where the Jaguar was kept. In reality this 'garage' was an old barn which was now being used as a garage. It had wide old cobb walls and I knew there was a hollow section at the top of one wall where they could be stored. Longer term, I would create an underground bunker for them and store them in such a way that a metal detector would not locate them. They needed of course to be accessible. This would require some further thought.

Clothing: I had to assume that I might be video recorded by CCTV on any of my missions. In addition to the coat with the bloodstains, I would dispose of the coats trousers and shoes worn on each killing mission. A bonfire in my bin incinerator was called for and then the ashes disposed of. I regularly had fires to clear garden rubbish so if noticed a garden fire would be of little interest to the neighbours. I would replace the trousers and shoes with new, and overcoats would be purchased from charity shops. On the basis that I might be videoed in future a bright coat could be useful once it was disposed of quickly afterwards.

Mobile Phone: It was important to leave no evidence on my phone. I had been careful so far to never use my mobile to research data on guns, people, protest groups, locations, train timetables or other information connected to my crimes I had left it at home on each of the two missions as I knew that the police could establish where it had been and its history of activity. Luckily, I received few calls so my absence on certain days would not be noticed. By leaving the phone turned on when away I could look to see what numbers had called while I was out. Unregistered Burner phones from which calls could be made cost £20 each and the phone could be disposed of after each mission.

Face and Hair: I have my hair in a layered bob cut with a steely grey colour which I feel suits my age. However, I could be accurately described by anyone who saw me. The blond wig and red-framed glasses I had purchased and used would need to be supplemented with different coloured wigs with longer hair and different framed glasses which would substantially change my appearance in a variety of ways. This would mean another visit to a salon in London where there are wig experts, and I would be anonymous. I do not normally wear glasses so a variety of framed pairs would each alter my facial appearance. This was as far as my disguise needed to go.

Gun: The pistol had now been used to kill two so it is highly probable that the police would establish that both bullets came from the same gun. For my next job it might be better to use the rifle. This meant learning how to maintain it, assemble and dissemble it and of course how to shoot accurately with it. Another visit to the 'shooting range' was called for.

Tiredness: The drive home from Cheltenham after a very traumatic evening was difficult and very tiring. I had almost nodded off a few times and could easily have crashed. It also involved getting home in the small hours of the morning which could draw attention to me. For future jobs I need to organise my travels to avoid long tiring days. Staying away from home was no inconvenience and could even be enjoyable if I chose nice places to stay. The downside to this was that hotels and guest houses needed your name and address and usually wanted to take an imprint of your debit or credit card at check-in.

Car: Sooner or later the police would link my car to the crimes. I needed to delay this for as long as possible. Petrol would be purchased from a variety of garages including some away from North Devon, but not close to the scene of any crime. Petrol should mostly be paid for in cash so that no debit card or bank account details would show where I had been. The Jaguar might have to be used at some stage in case my car was being watched. I would need to examine the car regularly to ensure that no tracker device was fitted. The car would need to be cleaned internally and externally regularly to ensure that no trace of any crime could be found on it.

Fitness: I need to be much fitter than I am now. I need to be able to walk considerable distances and to be able to run if the need arose. I also need to brush up on my cycling skills as walking and cycling were both good activities for getting and keeping fit. I determined to walk or cycle for an hour every day. I would also start doing stretching exercises daily to ensure that my arms and legs were toned to be flexible and agile. There were Yoga groups in Barnstaple and I would explore joining one of these.

Daughter and Son: I need to ensure that neither Anne nor Simon became in any way suspicious of my activities. I would phone them both as regularly as usual and the visits must continue. I would travel to Australia in March next year as planned and Simon and family would come to stay with me as planned after Christmas and again in the summer. Also, the neighbours must not be allowed to suspect anything from my behaviour and activities.

My friend Tom: Tom knew my right-wing views and he had also known my friend Sylvia and what had happened to her son. I need to make sure that Tom did not become suspicious of my activities and that my conversations with him gave him no reason to suspect my involvement in anything illegal.

There was much work to be done.

Chapter 11 - December 2022

Having hidden the guns away in the lock-up garage, I decided to purchase an air rifle which required no licence and could be used in the garden for target practice. I needed to become a marksman and felt that practice with an air rifle would help me to achieve this. The air rifle made minimal noise when fired – a loud click, but not enough to alert anyone. If a neighbour should chance upon me firing, I would explain that I planned to use it on any rats seen on the property, a problem that affected the village every winter. I set up targets in the garden and fired dozens of pellets at them every day from a distance of about one hundred metres. Within days, I had become a very good shot and could hit a target within a few seconds of lifting, aiming and firing the rifle. The neighbours showed no interest in this activity, if indeed they could even hear it.

I made plans for another visit to Exmoor. On the day before, I recovered both guns from the garage and cleaned and oiled the pistol. With the help of a YouTube video, which I had studied in the library, I took the rifle apart and re-assembled it three times. For the trip to Exmoor, I had it fully assembled as it would be difficult to assemble it whilst sat in amongst the heather. I would sling it over my back and wear a loose overcoat and backpack to hide it.

The rifle is an SA 80 L85 Variant, designed by Heckler and Koch and used by the British army since 1987. With a weight of 5 Kilograms, it measures 785 millimetres in length with a barrel length of 518 millimetres. It is fitted with a telescopic scope and a 30 round detachable magazine. For the less technical it is quite heavy, has a rapid-fire action with 30 bullets in the magazine and is accurate to 400 metres (1300 feet).

The barrel can be disassembled from the gun which reduces the length and makes it easier to carry.

The trip to the same valley in Exmoor as used before went well. I met no-one either getting there or returning and felt confident that I had not been seen. For the rifle, I set up targets about 250 metres away. By the time I had fired one hundred shots, I was hitting the target most times and was pleased to find that I had hit the bullseye six times. My daily practice with the air rifle had prepared me well. I also fired about one hundred shots with the pistol and was satisfied that my steadiness and aim were continuing to improve. Despite the two hundred shots echoing up and down the valley nobody came to investigate.

Chapter 12 - December 2022

On 14th December in Southampton, a young female police officer was injured after her police car was deliberately rammed by a teenage driver she was trying to pull over. The teenager had rammed her car at speed forcing her off the road and down an embankment. Her car overturned three times and finished back on its wheels. By an extraordinary stroke of luck, she escaped with just a broken arm and some cuts and bruises. Looking at the remains of the car in the newspaper it was amazing that she had not been killed. Needless to say, the young male driver did not stop to help the injured woman.

She was able to call for help, give the registration number of the car and the location. Within ten minutes the car was spotted and the driver arrested.

He was charged the following day with dangerous driving, attempted manslaughter and leaving the scene of an accident. He was bailed because he was about to start a new job as a trainee fireman, and the policewoman was not seriously injured. The public reaction to this was outrage.

There needs to be a strong deterrent against thugs or criminals attacking police officers.

I decided to see if I could get this young man's address (he had already been named in the papers). On a visit to the library, I looked up the local Southampton newspapers and to my surprise his name and address were openly published. His name was Alan Dudley. There was also a photograph of him which showed him to be a distinctive character. I would recognise him if I saw him.

I decided to pay a visit to Southampton and check out his address.

On 22nd December I drove to Southampton avoiding motorways and ‘A’ roads as best I could and had no trouble finding his address. He lived in a housing estate in a semi-detached house on a road with houses an both sides. There was a fair amount of traffic using the road. It was early afternoon and there were several children and young people to be seen from the house. I walked slowly past the house and continued to the next left turn. Returned along the road walking slowly. Opposite the house, about four doors down there was a semi-detached house for sale which looked unoccupied. I would visit this house later in the evening.

I took a bus to the City Centre and after a couple of hours in the library I had a pleasant meal in a Chinese Restaurant

At around 7pm, I returned to the road of interest. It was now quiet with nobody out and about, but there was still heavy traffic using the road. On reaching the house for sale, there were no lights on in it which confirmed to me that it was unoccupied. I opened the gate, went up the footpath and around the side, leading to the back garden. Went to the end of the back garden and saw that there was no gate because the end fence simply separated two gardens. There was no lane in between. Returned to the back door and the adjoining window through which I could see a utility room which led off from a kitchen. The door was locked and so was the window. It was a Georgian style window with two frames and the window could be opened by pulling the upper frame down to create a top opening, or by lifting the lower frame upwards to create a bottom opening. The lock was a simple mechanism holding the two window frames together. I waited a few minutes to ensure that no-one had seen me and might come to challenge what I was doing. All was well. I then punched the window frame where the lock was and could feel it move. After another few punches the lock sprang open, and I was able to lift the window upwards. With the help of a wheelbarrow which I stood in, I climbed through the window and into the utility room. Not bad for a seventy-four-year-old.

The key was in the back door. I went upstairs to examine the two rooms that overlooked the target house. The smaller room had only a small top opening window. The larger room had a side opening window which when opened would give a perfect view of the front of the target house. The central heating had been left on by the estate agent, so the house was quite warm. Back downstairs I locked the utility room window (properly this time) and left by the back door locking it behind me and taking the key. It was unlikely that the estate agent would visit over Christmas but even if he did, he would put the missing key down to a colleague rather than a burglar and would not be able to get a locksmith until after Christmas.

Chapter 13

On Christmas Eve I attended midnight service in the village church and chatted with several of my neighbours. On Christmas Day I prepared a full festive lunch with roast goose, vegetables and gravy, followed by homemade Christmas pudding. Cooking a full goose for two was extravagant but what was not eaten would come to good use over the following few days. Tom came over for lunch at 1pm and afterwards we went for a walk around Wistlandpound reservoir. Tom then left for home at 5pm. At 6pm I left for Southampton and arrived there at around 8.30pm. I parked in a suburb, took a bus to the city centre and then another bus to the road where Dudley lived, I let myself into the unoccupied house unobserved, having locked the back door and put the deadlock on the front door so that if the agent came and tried to enter, he or she would be unable to get in.

I was well equipped for a long stay. In my shopping bag I had the unassembled rifle and ammunition, a camera tripod, binoculars, two flasks of tea and coffee, sandwiches, cold goose, salads, a pork pie, fruit and Christmas cake.

I took everything to the larger front room upstairs. There were no curtains on the window and the light from a streetlamp took the darkness from the room. I had to be careful not to be seen near the window.

The only furniture in the room was a bed and mattress. I brought a chair upstairs from the dining room and keeping well away from the window set about assembling the rifle and loading it. I then arranged the tripod about a metre from the window at an angle which would give a clear view of the target house through the side window when opened. I positioned the chair a few feet behind the tripod where I could have a good view of the target house through the main window. With the help of binoculars, I could clearly see anyone outside the front door of the target house. I would recognise the target if he appeared.

There was no activity that evening up to midnight. I made a pillow from my coat and went to sleep on the bed covered by a blanket. At 7.30am on

Boxing Day I took up my vigil again watching the house.

A couple of hours later a middle-aged man left the house by the front door.

Around midday a young man knocked at the door, and it was answered by a middle-aged woman. She invited the visitor in. I opened the side window about three inches and took up position with the rifle resting on the tripod at shoulder height. I held the binoculars in my right hand with them focused on the front door. I needed to be sure that it was him.

Two men came out the door. The second one was Alan Dudley. No doubt that it was him. I put down the binoculars and aimed the rifle. They both stopped with the door still open, and the woman appeared. I aimed for the side of his head through the scope and felt confident of a good hit. He then moved his head and his body. I put down the rifle and took up the binoculars. For the next five minutes they continued to talk animatedly with Dudley moving around all the time. I picked up the rifle and aimed several times, but Dudley would not stay still. I could not risk taking a shot and missing so had to wait. Dudley's friend left and he went back indoors. So near and yet so far.

The only other movement from the house that day was when the middle-aged man, presumably the father, returned at 6pm. I continued to monitor the house until 8.30pm by which time I was tired and frustrated and hungry. Decided to take a risk and let myself out the back door, went around the side, down the path to the gate and let myself out. I hurried down the road away from the house. I looked back a few times and all was quiet. I hoped that none of the neighbours had seen me. I walked to a Chinese Takeaway and ordered a meal to take back to the house. I knew that this was risky, but frustration and hunger prevailed, so I took the chance. I got back to the house slipped in the gate and around to the back door and let myself in without putting on any lights. I remained in the kitchen for ten minutes listening and watching to see if the neighbours on either side came out to investigate. Nothing.

Relieved, I went upstairs to my operations room. I had my meal in darkness with coffee and felt much better afterwards. There was little point in continuing to watch the target house that night as I would not shoot in darkness anyway, so I settled into bed.

At about 10.30pm there was a loud knocking at the door. I got up quietly and watched from the window. There was a police car parked at the gate. I could hear the back door being tried and then there was an attempt to force the front door open. I could hear male voices. After a few minutes, having failed to get an answer from anyone in the house or to gain entry two uniformed police officers left the house. They did not immediately get into their car but crossed the road to speak to a neighbour who was at her gate. After a conversation which was clearly about the unoccupied house the police returned to their car and drove away. I guessed that the neighbour had seen me enter the garden and walk around to the back and reported this to the police. The police might decide to report the incident to the Estate Agent the following day, but it was unlikely that they would get an answer from them two days after Christmas. However, I would need to be alert tomorrow to the possibility of a visit from the Estate agent.

After an hour, I settled down again to sleep. I tend to snore whilst sleeping so I wore an anti-snoring device which my dentist had made for me. This was like a set of gum plates which locked to keep my mouth closed whilst sleeping. I hoped that it worked perfectly as otherwise I might be heard by the people in the adjoining house.

The following morning, I took up my monitoring position at 7am. Shortly after 10am, the target, Alan Dudley answered the front door to the postman and they both started to chat together. I replaced the binoculars, opened the window a few centimetres, picked up the rifle, cocked it and took careful aim. This time Dudley remained perfectly still. Squeezed the trigger slowly and fired. I could see that he was hit. He was thrown to his side and went down onto the lawn.

I closed the window and set about dismantling the rifle, followed by the tripod. I packed everything including the rubbish into my bag, picked up the bullet casing and cleaned the room. I carried the chair back downstairs and put it in its original place. It took about five minutes to clear everything and leave the house, locking the back door behind me and taking the key. Only then did I take off the rubber gloves which I had worn since entering the house.

Now for the most dangerous part of the job. I went out the front gate, crossed the road and started walking slowly towards the target house. I was wearing a dark wig, dark-framed glasses, and a wine-coloured knee length overcoat buttoned up to the neck. The bag was a dark brown plain shopping bag. As I passed the house where Dudley lay in the garden, the postman ran out to me and asked if I had seen anyone as I came up the road. I said that the only person I had seen was a young man running on the opposite side of the road and in the opposite direction. I asked him if everything was alright. He said there had been an accident and that I should go home and not worry about it. I continued to the end of the road and turned right, hurried to a bus-stop and put down the bag. I arrived back at the car in less than an hour and took off for home. The trip took four hours using a circuitous route. I dropped the gun off at the lockup garage, changed my clothes and had a fire in the incinerator. The overcoat, trousers, shoes, gloves, glasses and bag were all burnt together with garden waste, papers and a box of firelighters. I tended the fire until everything was reduced to ashes. These would be disposed of tomorrow. I would also need to hide the wig. I then went to bed at 9pm and fell into a deep sleep.

The following day I attended a lunch in the Village Hall which was organised by the Women's Institute as a Christmas celebration. I chatted with several neighbours and felt satisfied that my comings and goings of the past few days had not been noticed.

I took a drive after lunch, disposed of the ashes in the River Barle and visited a few charity shops in a nearby town South Molton, where I purchased two overcoats two pairs of shoes, a hat and a wooden box. I also called in to the library and went online to see what the Southampton Echo had to say about yesterday's killing. There was a brief report along the lines of 'man shot dead – police are investigating'. Similar brief reports were in the inside pages of the nationals.

Home at 6pm. I put the wig, which was now washed and nicely combed, in a plastic waterproof bag, and this inside the newly purchased wooden box. Buried it in a freshly dug part of a raised bed in the garden with the top of the box about thirty centimetres underground.

I could now face the police if they came and not worry about them searching the house.

However, I was very aware that I was an amateur killer and that with modern technology, much of which I was unaware of, the police may be able to track me down.

I would probably end my days in prison.

Chapter 14

A week after Dudley's killing the Southampton Daily Echo ran a story about him based on interviews with his friends, teachers, the police and his father. Below is an extract from the article.

"Alan Dudley was nineteen when he died. He lived his whole life in Southampton and had always lived with his parents. He had a brother and a sister. After an uneventful childhood he became a difficult teenager. He was arrested several times for disorderly conduct, assault, stealing cars and unsocial behaviour. Although he never went to prison and was treated very leniently by the police several times, he developed a hatred of the police. His parents continually tried to get him to change his behaviour and to consider a sensible career, but they had little success. Eventually his father had warned him that unless he got a job and started behaving, he would be disowned and made to leave the family home. This had a sobering effect on Dudley, who applied for a job with the fire service in Southampton and was successful at two interviews. He had then served as a trainee fireman for a year in a temporary role after which he was allowed to apply for a permanent position with the force. He was successful in his interview for this and was told that he would be offered a permanent position as a trainee fireman within two months. His parents were delighted with this apparent reformation of Alan.

It was during the two-month waiting period that he stole a car for a joyride and was followed and flashed to pull in by a police car. He tried to outrun the police car but on the outskirts of Southampton the police car caught up with him and pulled alongside his car. He saw that the police car was driven by a female officer and instead of pulling in he deliberately forced her car off the road. This was witnessed by two pedestrians. Her car went off the road at an embankment and overturned three times landing on the roof. Miraculously, the officer was not killed or seriously injured and was able to crawl out of the car and radio for help. She suffered a broken arm and some scratches and bruises.

The police felt that Dudley must have seen her car go over the embankment and would have known that she was likely to be seriously injured. He did not stop but instead made his way back to near his home. A police car, which had been alerted to watch for the car spotted him and ordered him to pull in. This time he decided to obey, pulled in, and was arrested.

Chapter 15 - December 2022

On Thursday 29th December, my son Simon, his wife Charlotte and their eight-year-old daughter Leah arrived to stay with me for a few days, having driven down from their home near Blackpool. Leah is a beautiful and charming girl, and I determined to give her a good time whilst in Devon. The four of us visited The Milky Way, a country theme park about an hour's drive from home, to ride the dodgems and the roller coaster and to see a birds of prey show. We walked on the beach at Putsborough, we had a trip up and down the Lynton Cliff Railway and went on the Steam Train at Woody Bay. These are all located in North Devon and provided plenty of activity and interest for eight-year-old

Leah. We had a few nice meals out and I cooked some meals for them at home.

They stayed until Monday 2nd January and we enjoyed bringing in the new year together. Tom joined us for a meal on new-year's eve and Simon and Charlotte seemed to like him a lot.

I wanted Simon and Charlotte to feel that I was happy and contented with my quiet life in the country and felt sure that I had achieved this.

They could see that I had a good social life, that I maintained the house and garden well and that I enjoyed reading, gardening, cooking and watching TV. The last thing I needed was for them to feel that they had to keep phoning me every few days to make sure I was OK.

They left at midday, and I promised that I would visit them in April or May. They made me promise to come to them by train as they felt that it was too far for me to drive. I gave them this assurance.

Chapter 16 - March 2023

There have been several terrorist attacks in Britain over the past few years by radicalised Islamic terrorists A well-known case was of Anjem Choudry who successfully preached radical terrorism in the UK for several years before eventually being charged with inciting radical terrorism. The charges related to the proscribed organisation Al-Muhajiroun, a terrorist organisation whose aim is to establish an Islamic State in Britain and radicalise people. It took the police years to manage to stop Choudry's activities.

I read this week that another radical Islamic preacher, Amir Bukhari, was arrested by police last month on suspicion of preaching radicalism but was released through insufficient evidence. This man has been associated with preaching Islamic terrorism for a few years but has so far been successful at avoiding legal sanctions. Another Choudry in the making.

I decided to look into this person further and after extensive research in Exeter library I managed to establish his address as well as obtaining a good photograph of him. He lives in Reading, is a practising solicitor, and has a wife and two children. He was born in Great Britain and is a British national. He became involved in preaching radicalism whilst at university in England and had travelled to Pakistan a number of times. I was satisfied from my research that this man was bad and dangerous and that his activities would lead to a terrorist incident sooner or later.

It was time to check out where he lived and what if any security measures he might have in place.

On Monday 6th March I set off on a daytrip to Reading. Although it would have been relaxing to travel by train, I took the car as it would be easier to find the location driving rather than walking. I travelled by motorway and arrived in Reading around mid-day. I had established that his address was at Wokingham, seven miles from Reading. I found his road and house without difficulty and parked a few blocks away. The houses on the road had front and rear gardens. The front garden was about 10 metres from the gate to the front door and was quite exposed with just a low fence and no trees or shrubs. After a thorough search I could not identify a safe place from which to watch the house or from where I could use the rifle. There was no access to the rear gardens which backed onto a stream or small river. It would have to be a pistol job which would be very dangerous. The road was quite long, and the target house was in the middle which would make it very difficult to make a clean getaway.

I decided that this person could not be targeted at his house. I would need to do further research to establish where he worked and if his workplace would make a better place to plan a hit rather than his home.

I made the long drive home feeling tired and frustrated having wasted a day.

I made my second visit to Reading travelling by train rather than driving. By visiting the main library, I was able to establish where Bukhari worked. He was a partner in a small firm of solicitors which had its offices in a modern building located in a business park about a mile from the town centre. I took a bus to the business park, found his offices and studied the surrounding area. At 11am the area was quiet with little traffic and few pedestrians. I returned at 12.30 pm to find the place busy with many pedestrians. I guessed that most were employees on their lunch-hour taking a stroll to stretch their legs. After an enjoyable meal in a restaurant near the business park I returned at 5pm and strolled around the business park noting where there were CCTV cameras. It would be necessary to circumvent these if I returned.

Between 5 pm and 6pm many hundreds of cars left the business park and between 6pm and 7pm the number of cars slowed to a trickle. I saw that Amir Bukhari's offices had an underground carpark which was accessed from street level with a drive leading down to the carpark. The entrance for cars was guarded by a wide garage door, which opened when activated remotely from a car entering the carpark and then closed automatically after the car had entered or left. There was a CCTV camera over the centre of the entrance door. I noticed that between

5.30pm and 6pm the garage door was set to remain open after each car left as there was a steady stream of cars leaving. At 6pm the automatic closing system was reset and thereafter the garage door closed automatically as each car left.

I did not know which car was Bukhari's so shortly before 7pm I took a bus to Wokingham and walked to the road where he lived. As I walked past his house, I could see two cars parked on his driveway. The car nearest the road was a large grey Mercedes saloon. The car in front was a small saloon car and I could not see the number plate. I assumed that the larger car was Mr Bukhari's and memorised the registration number as I walked past the entrance.

Having taken a bus back to Reading station I was pleased that I only had ten minutes to wait for a train to Taunton station where I had parked the car. Arrived home at 11.30pm and went to bed exhausted. This reconnaissance business was hard work. Indeed my clandestine activities were gradually becoming a fulltime occupation

Chapter 17

On Monday 27th March I drove to Taunton and took a train to Reading using a return ticket. At Reading I walked to Caversham Bridge, less than a mile from the station, and hired an E-bike, with helmet and padlock for the day. I arranged to return the E-bike to the rental shop yard after they had closed and to post the padlock key through their letterbox. The rental shop staff were insistent that I pay with either debit or credit card as insurance that they could take payment for damage or non-return of the bike. I explained that I did not have a debit or credit card and would have to pay cash. I offered to leave a deposit of £200 as insurance against damaging the bike and that they could return this to me by post after the bike was returned safely. I gave them a false name and address. They agreed to this arrangement.

I had not ridden an E-bike before so to familiarise myself I spent the next hour cycling around Reading centre. The electric bike was operated by pedalling like an ordinary bike but with the motor on, it was easy to peddle and to cycle quite fast. I found that I had no difficulty in managing the bike in the town traffic.

For cycling I was wearing a bright yellow waterproof zipped jacket, navy trousers, and flat black shoes.

I was also wearing a light backpack in which I had my loaded pistol, a pair of blue framed glasses, a blond wig, a red jumper and a biographical novel to read on the train. Before heading for the business park, I purchased a large black umbrella which I secured on the cycle frame.

At 5pm I cycled to the business park wearing the wig and glasses and the cycling helmet. I had established that a CCTV camera monitored all traffic entering and leaving the business park. There was a pedestrian entrance gateway about 300 metres from the main gate with a footpath leading to the buildings in the park. This gateway also had a CCTV monitor. I parked and padlocked the E-bike near this entrance and walked into the business park holding the open umbrella in front of me. The camera would record my entrance but would only show a person with a large umbrella. The recording might however show that the person was a woman.

The building where Bukhari worked was about 400 metres from the side entrance gate. I walked past the building at 5.35pm and saw that the automatic entrance door was open to allow the office staff easy exit with their cars.

A car left the building and drove towards the main exit. I walked confidently into the open underground carpark with the open umbrella held in front of me shielding as much of my person as possible, and found the basement empty of people. There were about twenty cars parked, and I quickly located Bukhari's car. Opposite his car there was a concrete staircase leading up to an entrance to the offices on the ground floor. I quickly went under the staircase and hid behind two large wheelie bins stored there. From this vantage point I could see anyone going to their car without any danger of them seeing me. Over the next twenty-five minutes fifteen cars left the carpark leaving five belonging to people who worked late. At 6pm the entrance gate closed. Bukhari's car was still in place.

Over the next hour three more cars left the carpark. I noted with relief that as each car approached the exit gate it opened automatically without the driver having to aim a remote device at it. This would make my exit easier. At 7.15pm Bukhari descended the staircase and went to his car using his key fob to unlock it. He opened the boot of the car to put in his briefcase when I stepped out from behind the wheelie bins with the pistol raised and cocked. He heard me and turned to look at me. I was just three metres from him and recognised him from newspaper photographs. I levelled the pistol and shot him in the centre of his forehead. The sound of the shot was enormous as the garage acted as an echo chamber and enhanced the sound.

I retrieved the backpack, put the pistol in it and put it on my back. I then made for the exit with the umbrella open and held in front of me. As I neared the garage door it started to open automatically.

I walked calmly out onto the footpath, closed and folded the umbrella and headed for the side gate. There was nobody to be seen.

I walked quickly to the side gate, went through it behind the umbrella, unlocked the bike and cycled away from the business park. I took a circuitous route to the station and from there to Caversham Bridge where I padlocked the bike in the bike rental yard and posted the key through their letterbox. The walk to the station took just 10 minutes during which I disposed of the umbrella. I purchased a single ticket to Paddington in London and crossed to platform 10 for a fast train. Boarded the train at 9.04pm and arrived in Paddington at 9.35pm.

Here I changed my appearance by removing the wig and glasses and the yellow jacket and putting on the red jumper. The jacket wig and glasses were discarded in a waste disposal unit outside the station.

I purchased a return ticket to Taunton and the train departed at 9.30. The first stop was Reading and everything looked normal on the platform with no police presence. Only one further stop and arrived at Taunton at 11pm. From there it was a fifty-mile drive over Exmoor, and I arrived home at 12.15am.

Chapter 18

The murder of Amir Bukhari made national headlines. It turned out that a colleague who had stayed working until late had found his body at 9.30pm, more than two hours after I shot him. The colleague had not heard the shot but estimated that Bukhari had left his office at around 8pm.

There were no witnesses to anything unusual in the business park that evening and CCTV showed that no cars had entered the business park after 6.30pm. A woman with an umbrella had entered the side gateway at 5.30 pm and had not left again until 7.30 still using an umbrella. Police appealed for the woman with the umbrella to come forward to be eliminated from their enquiries. This unknown woman became the main suspect for the murder as it had not been raining that evening and the CCTV footage suggested that she was using the umbrella to successfully hide her face and appearance.

The police were extremely disappointed and annoyed that the CCTV camera over the entrance to the basement carpark was out of order and nothing was recorded on the evening of the murder. Apparently, it had not been recording for months.

The newspapers had various speculative ideas on who might have committed the murder and there was concern that it might trigger revenge terrorist attacks.

The police condemned the murder but, in reality, it had solved a problem for them.

The general consensus with the public seemed to be that as he preached violence it was not unexpected for him to meet a violent end himself.

The police would almost certainly have established that the bullet used on Bukhari matched those used in three other murders but had apparently decided to keep this secret at this point in time.

Lorna Cooper was very aware that the police would know that four murders had been carried out by one person and that the hunt to identify her would be intensified, with more and more police resources being utilised on the case.

Philosophically she decided not to worry about being caught. This was probably inevitable and worrying about it was pointless, as it would spoil her enjoyment of life. She would however try to leave as few clues as possible in order to delay the inevitable.

Chapter 19 - April 2023

On April 19th I left my car in a garage in Barnstaple for a service and MOT and took a taxi home. That evening, I watched some TV as usual and went to bed at 11.30pm. Although I sleep very well, I am a relatively light sleeper, and any noise will awaken me. Usually it's an owl hooting, a fox barking or a cat crying but, on this night, I was awoken at 2am following a crashing noise coming from the kitchen. I thought it might have been breaking glass but could not be sure. I listened carefully and heard further sounds coming from the kitchen area. Someone was in the house.

I got out of bed quietly and picked up the baseball bat which was kept in a corner of the room behind an armchair. This bat had been kept in the bedroom for many years by my husband and it had remained there after he died. I was pleased that at least I had some form of weapon but fervently wished that it was a gun.

Assuming the intruder was a burglar, I reasoned that he or she would visit each room, including the bedroom, looking for items of value to steal.

The bedroom door was partly open as usual so I could hear what was going on. The intruder spent a few minutes in the kitchen, and I could hear drawers being opened and closed. He or she then moved into the lounge and made considerable noise searching for things. Assuming that it was a man he must feel that there was nobody at home, which, if he knew that I lived alone and knew my habits would be a reasonable assumption as my car was not on the drive.

I decided that it was best to remain in my bedroom and let him come to me. The baseball bat was an awkward weapon and could not be used in the doorway as it would hit the doorframe if swung to hit him.

I quickly tidied my bed so that it would look unslept in and figured that when he came into the room, he would start his search in the bedside cabinet nearest the door. Alternatively, he would walk into the room and make for the drawer units against the wall on the far side of the bed. There was a wardrobe against the wall on the side of the doorway and between this wardrobe and the window wall there was a space less than a square metre but large enough for me to stand in and hide. I stood with the baseball bat held above my head and resting on my shoulder.

I felt very calm and had no fear. My escapades over the past year had hardened me to respond well to pressure. I knew that if I failed to hit the intruder with a first blow it was unlikely that I would get a chance of a second. I also knew that rather than counterattack and kill me he would more than likely panic and make a run for it. He would be more scared than I was, which would give me an advantage.

After a few minutes the intruder arrived quietly at the bedroom door. I could not see the door but could sense it opening. A person entered the bedroom and stood for a moment by the bed and then shone a torch around the room. I heard the drawer of the bedside unit opening and the room was illuminated by the reflection from the torchlight. I stepped out from the side of the wardrobe with the bat held above my head. As I moved towards him, he heard me and started to turn towards me. I swung the bat and hit him hard on the top of his head and he fell forward and lay still. His head was bleeding where I had struck him, and he certainly seemed unconscious. I stepped past him carefully, switched on the light and got two pairs of shoelaces from the bedside cabinet.

I tied the man's hands together at his wrists. Then I tied his legs together by his ankles in such a way that he would be able to shuffle along rather than walk. His jacket pockets revealed a mobile phone, a wallet and a set of car keys. I next turned my attention to his injury. There was no sign of him recovering consciousness and for a few moments I thought that I had killed him. Getting rid of his body would be no easy task. There was now a lump on his head and an open cut which was bleeding but not heavily.

I fetched a bowl of warm water, a flannel, a bottle of antiseptic and a roll of bandage. He was now groaning and regaining consciousness. I washed the wound, applied the antiseptic (which made him scream from stinging pain). The wound stopped bleeding, so I decided to leave it uncovered.

The man seemed disorientated and asked me where he was and what had happened. I told him that I had knocked him out with a baseball bat and that my next blow would kill him. He then realized what had happened, discovered that his hands and feet were tied, and became very fearful. He asked if I was going to get the police. I said that I had not yet decided to involve the police and that it would depend on his behaviour and willingness to answer my questions truthfully. He assured me that he would tell me anything I asked. I told him I had his phone, and my first question was for his password. He said his phone used face recognition and on holding the phone close to his face it opened.

The last thing I wanted was to get involved with the police on this or any other issue and given what had just happened, I could end up having my photograph appear in a newspaper or even worse to appear on TV. I decided not to involve them.

Over the next ten minutes I determined his name, address, wife's name, and a potted version of his life history. He was a repetitive burglar and had been to prison five times. I was able to verify some of his answers through his phone and was satisfied that he was truthful with me.

I helped him to his feet and took him to the kitchen. He could just about walk with his feet tied loosely together. I could see that he was not well following the blow, so I made him tea and he drank this with two paracetamol capsules. By now I was feeling sorry for him and found that I was liking him.

I said that I would not be calling the police and that I proposed to let him go provided he promised never to cross me again. He visibly brightened and assured me that he would never bother me again and that if I ever needed him to do something for me, he would be pleased to do anything to thank me for sparing him. I said that I might need him to drive me to places such as Bristol and he said that he would be delighted to drive me anywhere, anytime. I wrote down his name and telephone number and returned his phone, wallet and keys to him. He could not believe his luck. To be on the safe side I got him outside the house before cutting the lace tying his hands and told him that he would have to untie his ankles himself after I had gone in and locked the door. I watched him from the kitchen window as he did this and left, waving to me as he went up the drive.

As he left, I felt satisfied that I had stopped a burglary, avoided involving the police and finding a possible driver who would keep his mouth shut. I would test him on an innocent shopping trip and pay him well if he demonstrated that he would be safe, reliable, discreet and confidential.

I must be getting soft in my old age to have allowed a burglar who had invaded my property and my privacy to get off so easily. He will never know how lucky he was to escape with his life.

I boarded up the broken window with cardboard, cleaned the baseball bat and went back to bed.

My low profile remained intact.

Chapter 20 - June 2023

I was watching the tennis tournament at Wimbledon on TV and witnessed the behaviour of 'Just Stop Oil' protestors during the first week of the festival, when Court 18 was invaded twice in one day and pink ticker tape and cardboard jigsaw pieces were scattered over the court. I saw that the players and the audience were upset and alarmed by these incidents, which turned out to be just publicity stunts with little harm done. However, it was clearly a continuation of a promised campaign to disrupt and sabotage sporting events in the UK. The Aintree Grand National, the Epsom Derby and major cricket events had already been disrupted.

The Wimbledon protesters were arrested and were facing fines and possible imprisonment, but I felt that neither would be sufficient punishment as the organisation was being funded by rich supporters and all the activists were happy to go to prison which they would regard as a badge of honour. Again, I felt that the 'Just Stop Oil' campaign, which was aimed at convincing the government to stop issuing fresh licences for oil exploration in the North Sea, was ludicrous and self-defeating as all it could achieve would be to make Great Britain less self-sufficient in oil and more dependent on imports from countries like Russia or an Arabic nation.

A few days later my anger with 'Just Stop Oil' protesters was intensified when a group of them stopped the traffic on the North Circular Road in London and one of them glued his hand to the road. It took the police over an hour to clear part of the road for traffic and a further two hours to have an expert release his hand from the road without injuring him.

I decided that my next act of social justice would be against this protester.

It was not too difficult to obtain the address of this activist, a retired architect named Joseph Turner, who lived in Ipswich.

Having already dealt with a major funder of 'Just stop Oil' (a spin-off from Extinction Rebellion), it was now time to go for one of the protesters. These people felt that they were above the law. They needed to be told that there might be a big price to pay.

Ipswich is about 350 miles from North Devon, a very long drive, and even longer avoiding motorways. This would have to be a train journey. I would do a reconnaissance trip first.

Leaving my car visible on the drive, I took a taxi to Barnstaple and from there a train to Exeter. Then a train to Paddington a tube ride to Liverpool Street Station and finally a train to Ipswich. At each station I checked as carefully as I could if there were CCTV cameras in operation and if there were any metal detection checks on passengers. I was wearing a blouse and smart business suit and smart shoes. My overcoat, which was one of my recent purchases, was mustard coloured and looked expensive. I wore make-up which I hoped made me look ten years younger and at each station I walked quickly and purposefully to give an impression of someone on business. I carried a tan leather top-opening briefcase, which contained a few stationary items, an Apple Mac laptop, and a small handheld recorder. If I was subjected to a metal detector and searched, the contents would pass as business related. I also had a light overnight bag with some personal clothing items and toiletries.

From home to Ipswich took seven hours which was tiring even though it mainly involved sitting. To avoid conversations with fellow passengers, I wrote letters to my children on the laptop or dozed. As it was late afternoon, I checked into a hotel in the town centre for the night and reserved a table for dinner at 7pm. This was relaxing and enjoyable and I was then in bed by 10pm.

From a security standpoint, I had encountered nothing on the trip to cause concern for the follow-up visit when I would be armed.

The following morning, I checked out and left my overnight bag with the porter and made my way by bus to the address of the target. I had seen his photograph in the paper but was not sure that I would recognise him. However, the electoral register showed that the only residents in the house were Joseph Turner and his wife. Having found the house I continued walking down the road until I came to a bus-stop which had a covered shelter and ‘pole’ seats. I sat in the shelter where I could watch the house without looking suspicious.

After a couple of hours, a man came out the gate and walked towards me. I studied my phone until he passed and then followed him from a distance. I was satisfied that he was Turner. He walked about a kilometre to a river bridge and then took a footpath by the river. I established later that it was the river Gipping. He was evidently out for a walk. I decided not to follow him as I would probably meet him, and it was too soon for that. I continued along the road to some shops from where I could look back to the bridge and see Turner when he returned. After about an hour, he appeared and made his way home.

I then took the river footpath and walked for two kilometres and back.

The path was well used as I met seven walkers and three cyclists on the first leg and eleven walkers and seven cyclists on the return leg. Also met a cruise boat with two people making its way along slowly. I passed three bridges each of which had an entry and exit for the river path. I explored the roads above each bridge and decided that the second one would suit my purposes best. It led to a busy crossroads where the left turn brought me to a bus stop. Within a few minutes, a bus arrived, and I was on my way to the town centre.

Back at the hotel I had lunch in their Italian restaurant, collected my bag and took a taxi to the station. Caught the 5.35 to Liverpool Street Station and then caught the 7.35pm from Paddington to Exeter. Eventually travelled on the 10.30pm to Barnstaple and got home by taxi at midnight. Was in bed asleep ten minutes later.

Chapter 21 - July 2023

On a beautiful day in July my friend Tom and I went for a walk and a picnic on Exmoor.

Tom, who is ex-army has right wing views fairly similar to mine. Our conversation ranged over many of the difficulties of modern society including illegal immigration, shoplifting, drug addiction, protest movements and burglary. We agreed that in general the penalties for such crimes were inadequate. During our conversation Tom asked for my view on the death penalty. Without hesitation I said that I was against it for most crimes but that I would like to see it re-introduced for pre-meditated murder and for treason. Tom said that he was surprised at my response as he would favour introducing it for a variety of crimes such as people trafficking, drug distribution, and terrorism.

We then had an interesting discussion about using reparation as a punishment for certain crimes. We felt that if burglars, shoplifters, and fraudsters had to make cash reparation for the value or cost of their crimes, with the risk of heavy jail sentences for non-compliance, it would be a much greater punishment and deterrent than the current system of community service or short jail sentences. The principal of reparation could even be extended to making disruptive protesters pay for the disruption they had caused.

We finished our discussion by agreeing that it would be pointless to try and present our ideas to government as the present flawed way of administering justice was so embedded that we would not be listened to.

After a glorious day walking and picnicking we drove home, and Tom dropped me off at 7pm.

Chapter 22 - July 21, 2023

I arrived in Ipswich at 5pm and checked into a different hotel from the one used before. The journey had been uneventful despite the fact that I was carrying a pistol in my overnight bag. I planned to be on the river footpath by 10am the following morning. If Turner was a creature of habit, he would use the footpath in the morning, but if not then I would stay in Ipswich for a few days and stakeout the river footpath each morning and afternoon. There was also the difficulty that I could only act if the coast was clear of walkers, onlookers or boats when Turner came my way.

The following morning the weather was fine, and I neared the bridge at 10am. I went up onto the bridge, and using binoculars, I was able to look back down the footpath for several hundred metres. In between doing this, I walked along the road to the crossroads and timed the buses for the town centre. There was one about every fifteen minutes.

There was no sign of Turner all morning, so I had to maintain my vigil for several hours. I was uncomfortably aware that somebody would notice me hanging around the area and could later remember enough to identify me. At 3.10pm I spotted Turner coming along the footpath, about 400 metres from the bridge.

There were no walkers on the footpath on his side of the bridge.

There were two walkers on the footpath, about 500 metres on the footpath on the other side of the bridge coming towards it. On the bridge where I stood there were no pedestrians, and I had noticed over the past five hours that pedestrians seldom looked over the bridge at the footpath.

It seemed that it would be safe to move. The walkers would not reach the bridge for several minutes and hopefully would not be alerted by a gunshot sound, in the distance.

I went down some steps from the bridge and started walking quickly towards Turner. I reach him about two hundred metres from the bridge and we both said hello as we passed. I reached into my bag, put the bag on the ground, cocked the pistol and turned to follow him. He heard me approaching, stopped and turned. I was about four metres from him. Without hesitation, I aimed at his chest and fired. His look of horror was shocking as he fell. I then fired another shot aiming at his head. He had fallen very close to the riverbank, and I rolled him into the river. This would not hide his body, but it would take several minutes for rescuers to recover his body and establish that he had been shot.

I recovered my handbag, put the gun inside it and hurried back towards the bridge. There were no onlookers. Once on the bridge, I crossed the road to see where the two walkers were. They were still about three hundred metres from the bridge and were clearly in no hurry. The noise of the shots had not alarmed them. I walked at a leisurely pace to the crossroads and the bus-stop. After just three minutes a bus arrived and took me to the town centre. Collected my overnight bag from the hotel and took a taxi to the station. A train to London was due at 5pm, which gave me twenty minutes to have sandwiches and coffee in the station buffet.

I reached Liverpool Street Station at 6.30 pm and Paddington Station by 7.10pm. The 7.35 Plymouth train reached Exeter at 10.30pm. I decided to break the journey and checked into a small hotel by Exeter station. Did not sleep well as the events of the day kept going around in my head. For the first time I felt pangs of guilt over what I had done. Had a very enjoyable English breakfast, caught a train to

Barnstaple at 10am and reached home by 11.30am.

Chapter 23 - July 2023

Over the next week, I spent many hours contemplating what I had done.

Having killed five people, I was now a serial killer. Each act had been a serious crime, and combined was mass murder, which would carry a life sentence with no remission, if caught. People would look upon me as a monster and would rejoice when I was locked up for good.

On the other hand, there would be many who privately and sometimes publicly would applaud what I had done.

Drug dealers facilitated the availability and widespread distribution of illegal drugs, which ruined the lives of thousands every year. There was a widespread perception by the public that the police were unable to get sufficient evidence to convict the top drug dealers and that these people continued to live the high life while addicts were suffering and dying.

The media reaction to the death of Boland in Taunton last year put the emphasis on his drug-dealing record rather than sadness at his passing.

Again, the reporting of the 'Just Stop Oil' activist linked his death to his protesting activities and the distain and contempt the public had for their disruptive behaviour.

The media reaction to the killing of the wealthy donor to 'Just Stop Oil' speculated that the killer might have been someone with a hatred of the protest movement and each newspaper pointed out that a large proportion of the population were disgusted with 'Just Stop Oil' and their activities and had little sympathy with their supporters.

I considered my feelings about the act of killing. I was convinced that the only satisfaction I got from a killing was a belief that the person deserved to die and that their death would act as a deterrent to others. I did not enjoy the physical act of killing and certainly did not want my victims to suffer pain or torture. I always wanted them to be killed instantly with the first bullet and hopefully to die without prolonged suffering.

Having read a few books about serial killers I was aware that they usually enjoyed the act of killing, that they became very arrogant and gradually became careless leading to their identification and capture. I felt that I did not have these traits.

Chapter 24

Joseph Turner was 67 when he died. According to the Telegraph he was born in Ashford, Kent to wealthy parents. He went to private schools followed by an Architectural Degree Course at the University of Sheffield, which he passed with honours. He then went on to qualify as an Urban Planner.

His career as an Urban Planning Architect involved several jobs with county and city councils and a firm of urban planners. He was excellent in his job in a technical sense but had poor people skills. He was a constant complainer and failed to develop any managerial skills. As a result, he always failed to progress upwards within each organisation he worked for and remained at lower levels throughout his career. He always earned a good salary and eventually retired with a good pension.

In retirement he became a protester with several protest groups but felt most at home with the 'Just Stop Oil' movement where he could indulge his love of complaining and participate in society disruption activities, which apparently satisfied his feeling that society had failed to recognise his talents and somehow let him down. He had a genuine affinity with the aims of the group but it
seemed likely that his real motivation real was to satisfy his need to complain.

Turner was married to Gloria for 40 years and they had no children. They liked to travel and had been to many places throughout the world, and they were content with one another.

As his murder was as a punishment for his ‘Just Stop Oil’ protests this could be seen as excessive and unwarranted, considering that his disruptive activities had not actually physically harmed anyone. On the other hand, he had participated in several disruptive protests with no consideration for the inconvenience and annoyance he had caused thousands of people.

Chapter 25

The media had not yet linked the five deaths as likely to have been caused by the same person, but I felt that it was only a matter of time before they did. The police would have connected four of the deaths through the make and markings on the pistol bullets but had apparently decided not to make this public at this point in time.

When I made the decision to embark on my vigilante activities, I knew that, if caught, I would be given a life sentence in prison. I was quite prepared for this as I am seventy-five years old and probably do not have many years of life left. My normal life's work was over. I had had a long and happy marriage, reared and educated two children and been a law-abiding (until recently), tax-paying citizen.

Having become a retired widow, I could spend my last few years leading a quiet life, gardening, reading, watching TV, visiting my family occasionally and cooking nice meals.

Alternatively, I could leave my mark on the world by ridding society of people who are anti-social and a drag on humanity, whilst at the same time sending strong warnings to others that there can be retribution for acts of damage to society. I would also be giving a message to government that unless they got a grip on lawbreakers the public might start taking the law into their own hands.

Whilst being willing to accept my punishment if caught, or even to die getting caught, I would do everything in my power to cover my tracks and leave no clues. I would try to ensure that in the event of being identified there was no evidence in my home, or on my property to provide the police with sufficient evidence to convict me.

After days of contemplation and philosophising, I concluded that my vigilante activities were worthwhile and that I was making a valuable contribution to society.

Having read the Telegraph Article on Turner I agreed that to kill Turner for his disruptive protesting was harsh, but I felt that the only way to get a message through to the protest movement was to make an example of one of them. Turner was the unfortunate victim of this decision.

To salve my conscience a little I decided that I would send Turner's widow a gift of money which would hopefully ease her pain a little and make her life more comfortable. I would send her £10,000 in a few months' time. Each time I used my debit card to pay for groceries I would ask for £100 cashback and would then save this cash until I had £10,000. This would ensure that all of the cash would be untraceable as it would be a mixture of used notes.

Meanwhile I would continue to identify, target and eliminate deserving individuals.

Chapter 26 - August 2023

From the newspapers, I was able to identify potential targets and also to read any reports or editorials about the people I had killed.

During August, I read about a notorious gangster in Ireland who had been shot and injured during a police raid on his house in County Meath and had been taken to a hospital in Drogheda, where he was recovering under police guard after an operation to remove the bullet. His name was Adrian Reilly, and he was considered to be a major gangland boss running a network of drug smuggling and distribution and was suspected of involvement in a number of gangland murders. It was considered by the media that much of the heroin sold in the UK was smuggled in from Ireland and that he was the main organiser of the trade. The Irish police (Garda Siochana) had been trying for years to get enough evidence to convict him and get him sentenced to a long stay in prison, but he was well organised, elusive, and had a team of expensive lawyers to keep him clean. I had read reports about him several times, reports which did not seem to bother him.

Although the Gardai had him under arrest and apparently had sufficient evidence to charge him with crimes, the legal process would probably take years, and his legal team would probably get him off. They were already demanding that he be released on bail, and it was likely that this would happen.

I became very interested in him and although there would be complications and huge risks, a plan gradually grew in my mind on how I might eliminate him. His death would be welcomed both in Ireland and the UK.

The difficulties of carrying out a hit in Ireland might be too great but it would do no harm to take a trip to Ireland to establish if it could be done.

There was no way of knowing how long he would be in hospital before being released and either taken to prison or bailed. Because an advance reconnaissance trip would take a few days and then preparing for a second trip would take some more days, I decided that there could only be one excursion, and it would have to be within the next few days.

The first and most obvious problem was how to get a pistol and ammunition into Ireland and then back into the UK, without getting caught.

Considering there was no indication that my car had been identified by the police as being of interest in connection with the three killings where the car was used, I decided that my Irish venture would be carried out using my own car. The alternative of renting a car was ruled out because I would have to show and give details of my driving licence to the rental company and would have to pay by debit or credit-card, which would leave a trail back to me. If I tried to hire a car paying cash, it would arouse suspicion about me and trigger awkward questions, and I would still have to give details of my driving licence.

The same problem could arise when paying for a ferry to Ireland, but I had a plan on how to pay with cash rather than a card.

Having decided to take my car, I had to decide where to hide the pistol within it, where it would not be found during any border checks. After ruling out many places in the car or the boot, I raised the bonnet and studied the layout. There was very little room for hiding the pistol.

I noticed that the car battery was housed in a four-sided plastic frame within which the battery sat and was then secured in place with a metal device. This device was a metal rod about 20 centimetres long. At one end the rod was bent at 90 degrees about two centimetres from its end and at the top of the rod it had two centimetres of screw tracks. The lower end gripped a metal plate on which the battery sat, and the top end went through a metal arm with a circular hole in it. Above this was a nut which was tightened to hold the battery steady in its casing.

I had the idea of placing the pistol and ammunition under the battery which would raise the battery about 3 centimetres. Then by raising the metal arm with the hole in it by 3 centimetres and getting a new rod 23 millimetres long, I could replicate the appearance of the secured battery without it looking different or odd.

Having retrieved the pistol from its hiding place I measured its width and found that at its widest point (the handgrip) it was 2.6 centimetres wide.

I had a new metal rod following the exact design of the original, but 2.7 centimetres longer, made at a local engineering workshop. Luckily, they were able to make the rod within two hours of my request.

I was able to unscrew the metal arm and using a drill made a new hole 2.7 centimetres above the original one and managed to secure the new arm at a higher level.

I released the battery and lifted it out of the car. It was much heavier than I had imagined but I could just manage it. I had cleaned and oiled the gun and wrapped it and two cartridges of ammunition in a tea-towel and placed it in the battery casing. I then lifted the battery and edged it back into its casing where it now stood a bit taller than before. I attached the newly made rod (having dirtied and oiled it to match its appearance with other metal items in the engine) and screwed it tightly so that the battery could not move. Having re-attached the positive and negative leads I checked that the engine would start and that the battery looked secure. I was very pleased with the end result. The newly raised battery looked as if it had never been touched since leaving the factory.

The next thing to sort out was money. I would need about £400 for the outbound ferry. The same in Euros for the return. Up to £500 for petrol, up to £600 for overnight expenses and £400 to cover meals and expenses. I visited my bank in Barnstaple and drew out £3000 In cash which was more than I expected to need. I would exchange sterling for Euros at the ferry port.

I knew that when I got to Drogheda, I would not take the car into the hospital grounds. I decided therefore to bring my bicycle on the back of the car strapped to a metal bike frame which I used when going for cycle trips around the Devon coast. It would also help explain to border officers why I was travelling to Ireland.

When packing my suitcase, I took into account that I could be away from home for up to a week. I also gave considerable thought on how to dress when I visited the hospital. The auburn wig would be used, and a new pair of glasses with coloured frames would be required. I would need a knee-length light summer jacket with deep pockets to carry the pistol, and a pair of slacks and smart shoes for walking and cycling. A pair of thin gloves would ensure that no fingerprints were left behind, but they needed to be such that they would not restrict me from using my hands and fingers.

A shopping trip to Barnstaple successfully secured everything I required including a burner phone, a tank of petrol, drinks, fruit and snacks for the journey.

Rather than take a ferry from Swansea to Cork, Fishguard to Rosslare,

Holyhead to Dun Laoghaire, or Liverpool to Dublin, I decided to take a much longer but hopefully safer route.

I would drive to Scotland and take a ferry from Cairnryan to Larne, and then drive through Northern Ireland to cross into the Republic of Ireland by road. Since The UK had left the EC (Economic Community) leaving complications between the UK mainland, Northern Ireland and the Republic of Ireland, I might be searched at Larne but was unlikely to be searched at the road border.

Finally, I packed my passport and driving licence and set off from home at 9am on 9th August. I had not told my neighbours that I was going away, and neither of my children knew I would be away either. I did however tell Tom that I was going on holiday for a week as I knew that he would be ringing me and wondering why I was not answering. I hoped that he would decide not to bother me whilst I was away. I left my mobile at home, turned on, and connected to a battery charger.

I drove for a couple of hours and stopped at Gordano Services in Bristol for a coffee having driven a hundred miles. From Bristol to

Cairnryan was a further 380 miles. I decided to get the long drive over in one day and stay in a hotel near the ferry port. The drive from Bristol took seven hours including two ten-minute breaks. Reached Stranraar (ten miles from Cairnryan) at 7pm and checked into a small hotel. Had dinner in the hotel and retired exhausted to bed. I had offered to pay my bill in cash, an offer that was gratefully accepted and I settled my bill that evening.

Caught the 9.30am ferry and arrived in Larne at 11.40am. Was waved through customs and then took a circuitous route to the Republic of Ireland border. Crossed the border on the A3 near Monaghan without incident and continued to Drogheda via Kingscourt and Ardee. I reached Drogheda at around 3pm and parked in a supermarket carpark on the Donore Road about half a mile outside town.

I put on the auburn wig and the glasses with matching frame. I cycled into Drogheda and made my way to 'Our Lady of Lourdes' hospital which was half a mile from the centre. It was uphill to the hospital, so I walked pushing the bike. Parking for bikes was free with stands near the main entrance. However, I went into the main carpark and put the bike against a tree and locked it.

The hospital was big and was made up of several buildings. I sat in a cafe in the foyer and had a coffee. The cafe had only a few customers and I engaged in conversation with the waitress. After a few pleasantries, I asked her if it was true that a famous gangster was a patient in the hospital. She said it was true and that he was under police guard. I asked if he ever came to the cafe for coffee. She laughed and said no, that he was quite ill anyway and was in G Block which was at the far end of the hospital.

I made my way to G Block and took the stairs to the fifth floor. I felt that it was probable that he would be kept as far away from the public and staff as possible and that the top floor would be a good starting point. The top floor which was accessible from the staircase was made up of offices all of which seemed empty. I walked down a long corridor at the end of which was a door on the left marked ‘emergency exit’. I opened this door and stepped into a small room with a second door marked ‘emergency staircase’. Opened this door by pressing a bar on it and stepped out onto an external metal staircase and looking across this I could see that it led to the ground at the back of the building. I re-closed the emergency door and made my way back to the main staircase. Closing the emergency door made a loud noise which I feared might attract attention, but nobody came out from any of the offices.

Went down to the next floor and stepped into an open area where there was a large sign saying 'No entry to patients or visitors. This looked promising. Ambled down a corridor and saw a man sitting outside a room. He stood up and approached me asking where did I think I was going. I acted bewildered and said I was looking for the mortuary. His tone softened and he explained that I was in the wrong building and would need to go back to the main lobby and get directions from there. He suggested that I use the lift to return to the ground floor and pressed a button to summon the lift. I thanked him and took the lift down. I left by an exit door and studied the outside of the building. Although it was daylight, I could see that there were lights on in only two rooms on the fourth floor adjoining where the man had been sitting. I guessed that my target was likely to be in one of these two rooms. I then checked that the fire escape staircase could be easily exited at ground level, which was the case and leading from it there was a footpath going in both directions around the building. The problem now was how to get past the guard outside the patient's door.

I retrieved the bike and cycled into town and out to my car on the Donore Road. Drove a few miles to an empty layby and retrieved the pistol. Put the battery back and re-connected the leads. The battery was loose in its casing, but this would not affect the cars drivability over short distances. It was now 3.30pm and I decided that attempting the job in daylight would be best, as I would depend on my age and frailty to divert attention from me.

I changed my shoes to black flat shoes with soft soles and heels so that I would make little sound in the building and could descend the metal external steps quietly. Put on a long-sleeved jumper over my blouse and then carefully arranged the wig and glasses. Drove back to the supermarket and parked near to a recycling skip. Finally, I put on my newly acquired jacket and put the loaded pistol in a deep pocket.

I cycled back to the town and made my way up to the hospital pushing the bike. Took the footpath around to G Block and put on a covid facemask before heading up the stairs. I had seen earlier that many patients and staff were wearing covid facemasks as a precaution against the ongoing chance of catching Covid in the hospital. Stepped out on the fourth floor and could see the chair along the corridor but not the guard. I had planned to march him at gunpoint into the room, but this was no longer necessary. Made my way quietly along the corridor, cocked the pistol and kept it in my pocket but with my hand gripping it.

At the door beside the chair, I turned the handle and stepped inside. My calculation had been correct. There was a patient in a bed, and I recognised him as Reilly. He was alone in the room. I approached a surprised Reilly and pulled out the pistol. He dived for his bedside locker as I shot him. My first shot hit his shoulder as he was moving, so I shot him again in the head and felt satisfied that this shot had been accurate and would be fatal. There was a spurt of blood but as I was about two metres from him, I avoided being splashed. Within three seconds of shooting him I went back to the door and out into the corridor where I came face to face with the same guard I had met earlier.

His hand was inside his jacket, presumably reaching for a gun. I levelled my pistol aiming at his face and ordered him to put his hands up which he did. I said ‘I have no quarrel with you and do not want to shoot you but if you make a wrong move or go for your gun I will kill you. Do you understand!” He nodded his head and kept his hands up high. I walked backwards about five metres towards the stairs still aiming the pistol at him. Saying "I have just done you a huge favour by killing Reilly." I lowered the pistol, turned right and entered the staircase.

To my surprise and relief, he did not follow me immediately. I still cannot fathom why he let me escape so easily. Perhaps it was shock, perhaps he had never shot anyone and could not bring himself to shoot me, or perhaps he felt that Reilly deserved to die and that he did not want to kill me or make me pay for the crime. Alternatively, he may have been afraid that if he followed me down the stairs, I would wait for him on one of the landings and kill him.

When I reached the main staircase, I went up to the top floor knowing that the police officer would expect me to go down the stairs. I entered the top floor which was as empty as it had been earlier in the afternoon and went quickly to the end of the corridor and into the room with the emergency exit. Let myself out onto the metal staircase, removed the facemask and descended to the ground at a leisurely pace but as quietly as possible. From there, I walked on the footpath back towards the main entrance but before I got there, I was able to cut across to the main carpark. Found my bike and unlocked it. Made sure there were no onlookers and removed my jacket with the pistol in the pocket, took off the gloves, the wig and the glasses and put them in a carrier bag which I had brought in the second pocket of the jacket. I then cycled through the carpark, left the hospital grounds, and headed for Drogheda town. It was downhill all the way to the river and then a level road to the supermarket where the car was parked. I put the pistol in the glove compartment, the jacket went into the recycling skip and the gloves in a waste-paper bin. Set off towards Donore and there turned right towards Slane. On reaching Slane I joined the N2 road towards Ardee and pulled into a secluded layby. Here, I lifted the bonnet, took the leads off the battery and lifted it out. Wrapped the pistol in a tea towel and replaced it in the bottom of the battery casing. Managed to lift the battery and fit it back in place just as another car pulled into the layby. Seeing a woman working on her car engine with the bonnet open the driver came over to see if he could help. I had no alternative but to tell him that a battery lead had become loose, and I was fixing it. He insisted on helping and secured the battery leads and the device to hold the battery steady. I was scared that he would notice that the battery was higher than it should be or that the locking device has been adjusted to a higher level. He did not notice that there was anything unusual. He commented on my English accent and asked if I was on holiday. I confirmed that I was in Ireland for ten days touring and cycling and that I lived in Bristol. He was a very nice man, and I thanked him profusely for his help.

When he drove off, I felt quite sick as I knew that I had left a vital clue for the police. Two people had now heard my

English accent, and one had a description of my car including the numberplate. I drove on towards the Northern Ireland border. Stopped on a bridge and flung the wig and the glasses into a river. I read somewhere that water would remove all traces of DNA if either item was ever found and examined. Hopefully this was the case.

At Castleblaney. I turned off the N2 and onto the R25, a minor road leading to the border. I expected to cross the border without being stopped.

However, before reaching the border, I was waved to stop by two Gardai whose squad car was blocking the road. They asked me to step out of the car and asked where I had been and where I was going. They were very polite but explained that they were searching for a woman who had committed a crime and that they would have to search me and the car.

I agreed willingly and submitted to a thorough search of my person by the female Garda whilst the male officer started on the car. He took the bike off the rack and asked me to open the boot. They took everything out of the boot and searched it thoroughly even lifting out the spare wheel to check under it. This had been one of my considered hiding places. They then searched inside the car, even checking the panels of the doors and the coverings on the seats. They then asked me to open the bonnet and thoroughly searched around the engine. Finally, the male officer lay down and pulled himself under the car to examine the underneath carefully. They found nothing.

They were, however, very suspicious of me. The fact that I only had a burner phone with no numbers stored on it caused concern. I explained that I only carried it at the request of my children so that I could call for assistance if I became ill or had a breakdown or an accident. They examined my driving licence and passport but did not write down my name and address,

Finally, they apologised for what they had put me through and let me drive on.

I realised that I was now in trouble. The Irish police knew my name and could probably remember my address. They knew my car registration number and worst of all they could identify me if ever shown a photograph.

As I had been in Ireland for less than a day, it would look very suspicious if I turned up at the ferry to return to the UK today.

I decided that I would have to stay for a few days to uphold my cover story that I was on a cycling holiday. I crossed the border, with no further checks or searches, and instead of heading for Larne, I drove to Armagh and checked into a hotel. Had a leisurely dinner and went to bed at ten. The evening news headlined the story of the killing in Drogheda and said that the killer was believed to be a woman aged about 50.

The following day, I checked out but got permission to leave my car in the hotel carpark. I cycled around for the day visiting the sights including Armagh Cathedral, which was magnificent. At 4pm, I returned to the hotel, collected my car and drove to Sligo, a journey of about 60 miles. This drive involved crossing the border into the Republic again. There were border guards at the crossing, but they were not interested in cars coming from the north and waved me through.

I stayed in a nice hotel in Sligo and again checked out in the morning but left my car in the hotel carpark. Had an enjoyable day cycling around Sligo town and along the Garavogue river. Left Sligo at around 4pm and drove to Derry in Northern Ireland. The border post was unmanned so I was able to drive straight through. Stayed two nights in Derry and relaxed and did some cycling. It was now five days since arriving in Ireland so I felt that it might be safe to head for home. Reached Larne in the early afternoon and purchased my return ticket.

To my amazement, I was able to drive onto the ferry without inspection or search. If the police were looking for an English woman driving an English registered car, then surely there would have been a check at the ferry ports. I spent the crossing wondering if I would be searched or arrested when we docked in Cairnryan. As I drove off the ferry I was simply waved through.

I spent the night in the same hotel I had stayed in on Wednesday night at Stranraar. Then, the following day I drove the 500 miles home with a few stops. I used the motorways and the link road and reached home by 11pm. Went to bed exhausted and slept like a top.

Chapter 27

Following his killing the Irish Times published a lengthy article about Adrian Reilly and his life of crime.

He was 47 when he died. Born in Crumlin in Dublin he had been in trouble with the police from the age of ten onwards. He was a violent aggressive boy who vandalised public and private property, indulged in shoplifting, burglary, physical assault and various other anti-social crimes.

As a teenager, he was sentenced to two years in a detention centre where he served eighteen months.

During his twenties he served two three-year prison sentences and served eighteen months for each one. Prison did not teach him any lessons or help him to stop his life of crime. On the contrary, he used his time in prison to create relationships with other criminals and to plan his future career as a drugs baron and gangland boss.

In his thirties he built up a team both nationally and internationally and concentrated on the importation and distribution of heroin. His heroin was sourced from sources in Turkey, Lebanon and Iraq and made its way into Ireland in a variety of ways. The favourite route was by sea where a motorboat, contracted to transport the drugs would land them on a quiet beach in the southwest or west of Ireland having picked up the goods from a ship seven or eight miles out at sea. The drugs would be landed on a pre-arranged beach in the early hours of the morning. The Irish navy comprises a fleet of six patrol vessels and the drug smugglers could track the whereabouts of these patrol boats and ensure that there were none in the area when picking up drug consignments from ships. Reilly's men would meet the motorboat to collect the goods. A second transport method was to hire a small yacht and sail the drugs from France to Ireland landing late at night at small un-manned harbours and quickly offloading the goods. The ships, yachts and landing places were continually changed which made it very difficult for the police or the navy to intercept drug loads as they arrived in Ireland.

The bulk heroin was then repackaged into saleable doses in re-sealable plastic bags. These were then sold by a network of dealers in Ireland and the UK. Smuggling the heroin into the UK from Ireland was easy using unmanned border crossings into Northern Ireland and then by ferry to the UK.

Reilly became very skilled at managing his team, administering his business and evading the police. He was ruthless with any of his team or any competitors who crossed him, where the penalty was death. He had employees who were willing to act as hitmen and the police believed that he was indirectly responsible for at least eleven murders.

He was married and was known to have various mistresses over the years, had three children and had a very stylish lifestyle with several houses, cars, and a luxury cruiser on the Mediterranean. His personal security was substantial with bodyguards and a variety of technological safeguards.

It was well known in Dublin that he was a gangland boss dealing in drugs. The police knew him, the media knew him (but were careful what they reported about him) and the people of Dublin knew about him. He accepted this as a badge of honour and was careful to ensure that there was never direct evidence of his activities to enable the police to convict him.

The raid on his house in County Meath, during which he was shot and seriously injured, took place in the belief by the police that a shipment of drugs had been delivered to his house. The police forced open his security gates and drove up to his house. Reilly foolishly reacted by stepping out of his front door brandishing a rifle and demanding that the police depart. When they refused to do so and said they had a warrant to search his house, he lowered his rifle and aimed it at the lead police officer. An armed officer standing by his car shot Reilly to protect his colleague. Reilly was taken to hospital under police guard and when his house was searched there was no sign of any heroin or other drugs, but two pistols were found. Reilly had no licences for the pistols or the rifle. He was charged and placed under arrest (whilst in hospital) for possession of firearms and attempted murder of a police officer. The police had established that one of the pistols had been used in an unsolved murder thus linking him directly to a murder.

Chapter 28

The following morning, I replaced the pistol in its hidden location in the building where the Jaguar was parked. I put the car battery in its original position and replaced the device to hold it in position with the original. I walked about 200 metres from the front gate along the road leading out of the village and hid the higher battery securing device in a hedge. I might need this again but could not afford to have it found on my property.

I picked up the post and the newspapers from the floor of the hallway. The papers would make interesting reading. There was nothing in the post except a few bills.

I decided to take a walk around the village to show the neighbours I was home. I chatted to a few and they did not remark on my absence. Arthur the postman, had noticed my absence and I told him I had been away for a few days holiday.

I was still amazed that it appeared that I had escaped so easily despite the clues I had left behind. Of course, it may be that the police now know exactly who I am and are simply putting a case together before arresting me. I looked forward to reading the Irish papers, north and south, to see how they had reported the killing of Reilly. I could not do this on my laptop or phone as these could become evidence.

Went to Barnstaple in the afternoon and spent a few hours in the library and read through all the relevant newspapers. The assassination of Reilly was reported as a daring attack and there was criticism of the Gardai for allowing it to happen. The officer on guard had reported that he had left his post for one minute for a comfort break, heard the shots and when he returned was ambushed by the assassin and held at gunpoint by a blond woman aged about 50 who was wearing glasses. He was forced to stand with his hands up while she walked backwards to the stairs. Rather than follow her immediately he had gone into the room to see if Reilly was still alive and needing help. Once he saw that Reilly was dead, he had radioed for help and then run to the staircase and hurried down to ground level. He had searched for the woman both inside and outside the block but failed to locate her.

I made a mental note to confirm that this was what had happened if caught and interrogated. There was no mention of my English accent. Either he had kept this to himself, or the Gardai had decided to keep this detail secret. Within thirty minutes of the killing, police checks were set up at all border crossings, at all ferry ports, at Drogheda Railway station, and on all main roads leading out of Drogheda. The main roads to Dublin got special attention with every car being stopped, and all cars with a woman driver or passenger being searched. The hunt was for a middle-aged woman with red hair and dark red glasses, carrying a pistol in the car.

The public were asked to assist in the search but to approach anyone matching the description with extreme caution as she was dangerous. There was nothing reported about my car being searched near the border. My decision to remain in Ireland for a few days had saved me from being searched at the ferry port and probably from being identified and arrested.

The media had somehow reached a consensus that the killing was a professional hit organised by his gangland enemies. Although embarrassed by the incident the Gardai did not seem to be putting substantial resources into finding the assassin. The English national newspapers gave the incident very little coverage and there was absolutely no suggestion that the Irish murder was linked to any English murders.

The Irish Times had focused on Reilly's life of crime and implied that if it was a gangland hit then it was rough justice and no loss to society.

Having had such a close brush with the law, I decided that I needed to tighten up on my security precautions and to try to learn lessons from the Irish adventure.

The guns still needed to be better hidden, and at the same time made more accessible. They needed to be stored away from my property so that a home and garden search could not uncover them.

On a neighbouring farm, about a mile from my home, there was an ancient barn which was used as a winter shelter for sheep during bad weather. It had no doors so was always open. I was familiar with this barn as I sometimes sheltered in it myself during winter walks. The barn had originally had a floored loft for storing animal feed, but this had long ago rotted away and only a corner of the wooden loft remained. There were no steps to this piece of the loft which was about a square metre in size and was inaccessible without a ladder. A low box could be hidden on this piece of loft in such a way that it could not be seen from the floor of the barn.

I already kept a blond wig in a box buried in the garden. I dug up this box and cleaned it off. I then collected the pistol, rifle and ammunition from the building in which the Jaguar was parked. I took the barrel off the rifle and was able to fit the rifle, pistol and ammunition, together with wigs and glasses in the box. Then I purchased a telescopic ladder. This is an easy to assemble ladder weighing 16.4 kilograms which extends to 6.2 metres. I was able to drive and park close to the barn and once I established that the coast was clear, I erected the ladder against the wall next to the remaining corner of the loft. I ascended the ladder and checked that the wooden loft piece would support a heavy weight by leaning on it. Perfect! I returned to the car, carried the weapons box into the barn, took it up the ladder with some difficulty and put it in place back against the wall and out of sight from the ground. I then got an old sack which I had brought and covered the box with it so that even if somebody could see that there was something up there it would look like some farming material. The box was also placed in such a way that I could open it and retrieve the pistol or rifle and ammunition without having to take down the box. Having satisfied myself that the box was safe and well-hidden, I returned the telescopic ladder to the boot of the car. I then checked that the floor of the barn which was covered in dust and straw did not show any footprints or sign that I had been there. In future I would take a brush with the ladder when accessing the guns to sweep the floor before leaving.

The main risk with this hiding place was of someone disturbing me whilst accessing the box. This risk was minimal as any future visit to the box would take about two minutes and I could check in advance that there were no walkers or the farmer in the vicinity.

Back home, I went through my clothing to see if any items could be identified from my travels and bagged up a number of items and took them to a civic waste disposal centre in Bideford and put them in the garment container.

I put all back copies of newspapers out for bin collection the following day, and checked over the car for anything that would give a searcher a clue.

Chapter 29 - September 2023

On Tuesday September 14th, I flew to Australia to see my daughter Anne and her family. I drove to Exeter Airport and flew to Paris. From Paris, I flew business class to Perth, with a stopover in Singapore, and had a pleasant journey. Anne met me at Perth airport and from there it was a two-hour drive to their farm. My son-in-law Bernard is a very charming man and always makes me feel very welcome. My two grandchildren, Tyler and Rebecca, are beautiful children, and I love them dearly.

For the first week, I relaxed and wound down after all my activities back home. We had barbeques and ate outdoors. We went to the Zoo, to the beach, to the desert and around the amazing farm. My family have a great lifestyle there. They work hard but live well and they were very happy. It was Anne's birthday during my second week there and as a special treat I took Anne, Tyler and Rebecca on a trip to Sydney on the other side of Australia. Bernard had to stay and look after the farm, and I could see that he was sorry he could not come with us.

We flew from Perth to Sydney on Jetstar which cost £1500, and the flight took four hours which gives an idea of how wide Australia is. We stayed in a nice hotel and the following day did a sightseeing tour of the city. That afternoon, we departed from Central Railway Station on the Indian Pacific to Perth. This was a four-day journey crossing Australia from East to west, covering 4000 kilometres, and renowned for its luxury and being one of the great rail journeys of the world. The trip for the four of us cost £5000 but I felt that I could afford it. The trip would be educational and adventurous for the children, and it might be the last adventure together that we would ever have.

The train journey was incredible and was easily the best journey I have ever had. The train was luxurious with air conditioning, soundproofing, and had no expense spared on the décor and furnishings. We had three cabins, a double for Anne and Rebecca, a single for Tyler and a single for me. The beds were comfortable and the cabins each had a shower, washbasin, bedside reading lamps, chair and dressing table and a TV. The experience of being rocked gently to sleep by the moving train was so luxurious.

The scenery as we crossed Australia was varied and fantastic. The landscape was mainly arid and semi-desert with sparse growth of grass and trees. Homesteads and farms were only to be found close to the few cities and towns we encountered. The train stopped just once each day, at Broken Hill, Adelaide, Rawlinna and Cook, where we were able to stretch our legs and explore for a few hours.

Broken Hill is an old mining town where we visited the Living Desert Reserve, which has twelve spectacular sandstone sculptures lining a hilltop and giving a wonderful view over the desert. Adelaide is a city located in a wine region and here we visited the impressive Art Gallery of South Australia and had a luxurious meal. I drank a little too much wine followed by a Cognac and could barely totter back to the train. The children were highly amused at this, but I don't think that Anne was too impressed. Rawlinna is a small railway town best known as Australia's largest sheep station, where we had an evening stop and enjoyed a luxurious meal sitting out under the stars. The last stop was at Cook, an old abandoned, railway town with only a handful of residents. It is used as a swap over town for the train crews. We had a few hours here to explore the old town having been given a map as a guide. These four stops were a great way to break up the journey and gave us an insight to parts of Australia that most tourists never see.

This trip was good for Tyler and Rebecca and as it taught them how huge their country was and gave them a great insight to its landscape. For me, the four days were magical. I gave little thought to my life of crime and enjoyed the company of Anne and the children. Back in Perth the last week of my holiday flew past, and it was with great sadness that I said goodbye to Anne, Bernard, Tyler and Rebecca, as I felt that it might easily be the last time I would see them.

The flight home was smooth and luxurious, but I could not help worrying that the police may have caught up with me whilst I was away. When I arrived home, I went through all the Telegraph newspapers which had continued to be delivered to the house every day.

It turned out that my worries were unnecessary as there was little in any of the papers for me to be concerned about.

Chapter 30 - November 2023

An activity which featured regularly in the news this year was shoplifting. The police evidently looked upon shoplifting as a very minor crime, which should be controlled by the shopkeepers themselves. This was of course a ridiculous stance to take as store security staff did not have the power or authority to arrest and charge shoplifters and had to let anyone caught go if the police failed to attend to arrest them.

As a result, shoplifters had become emboldened and organised and had elevated shoplifting to a new level. A group of thieves would enter a supermarket with prams, bags and backpacks, and load up with spirits, wines, expensive food items, and electrical goods including TV's, Radios and Microwaves. A current favourite was the new Air-fryers. One of the team would deliberately create a distraction and, whilst the management and security staff dealt with this, other members of the gang would leave the store with their haul. Threatening behaviour was used against the staff to stop them from intervening and once out of the store they were free to make off with whatever they had taken. A raid like this could cost a store several thousand pounds.

The major supermarkets were trying to resolve this epidemic as best they could with better security cameras, face recognition, barring known shoplifters and other security methods but, in reality, they were unable to combat the organised gangs and had to suffer the resultant losses. These losses were then passed on to the customers in the form of higher prices which means that we are all paying for the shoplifter's thefts.

I was appalled at this and felt that the organised shoplifters needed to be given a sharp shock. Bristol was considered to be one of the worst cities for these gang attacks so I decided to take a look at some of the larger supermarkets there and see if I could come up with a viable plan.

On the first day trip to Bristol, I visited twelve large supermarkets to assess their suitability to me. All twelve were rejected for the same reason. I was looking for a supermarket which had buildings in front of it which could provide a vantage point for a stakeout. All the supermarkets visited had large shopper carparks in front of them and all were located away from built-up areas. I finished in a disappointed mood and drove the 100 miles home.

On the next trip, I altered my search to medium sized supermarkets on high streets in shopping areas. Eventually, I located one on the Gloucester Road about two miles from the city centre. The street was wide with shops on either side with offices or living accommodation above most of them.

The store I selected was on a crossroads corner. There was nowhere suitable for my purposes on the main road but on a residential side road I saw that several of the houses there would give me a clear view of the supermarket entrance from an upstairs window. The houses were mostly divided into flats and one of them had a flat to let on the first floor. The distance from this house to the supermarket entrance was about 200 metres which was well within the range of my rifle, and my capabilities.

I telephoned the letting agent whose number was on a placard in the garden and asked if they would consider letting the flat for one month only. I would pay in advance and would be happy for potential tenants to be shown the flat while I was there. The agent seemed keen. I explained that I had to return to my home in Wales the following morning and asked if they could possibly show me the flat today. The agent agreed and we arranged to meet at the address in an hour.

This gave me just enough time to visit a salon in Bristol that sold wigs, which I had found on Google earlier. I picked and paid in cash for an auburn wig which looked good on me and had it trimmed to suit my face. I was now keeping £2500 in cash in the car to avoid having to use cash machines through which I could be traced. I also purchased a pair of glasses with auburn frames to set off the wig and create a face disguise.

The letting agent was a young man named Mark. I liked the flat, which was semi-furnished as it gave an uninterrupted view of the supermarket from the lounge bay window which opened on both sides. The flat included a residents parking permit to park on the road outside. The agent explained that for a one-month tenancy he would have to charge three month's rent which would be £2700. I opened my handbag and took out £2000 in £20 notes and said I was prepared to pay this amount there and then in cash. He said he could not agree to this but would settle for £2500. I put the cash back in my bag and thanked him very much for his time and stood up to leave. He agreed to the £2000 and I paid it over. We completed some paperwork, and I gave a false name and address. He wanted proof of identity, but I did not have any with me, so he dropped this request. I gave him my mobile number (my burner phone) and said he could phone me anytime he wanted to show any potential tenant the flat. If I was not there, he could let himself in. He gave me the key and wished me a happy month. I explained that I was attending an Open University Course and would have a busy month. The flat was heated, had a well-equipped kitchen, a TV and two armchairs but did not have a bed. I would purchase an airbed and pump and a sleeping bag so that I could stay overnight from time to time.

Chapter 31

Time was of the essence. The first priority was to have another training session with the rifle. I had to perfect my aim from 250 metres and ideally be able to hit a moving target. I felt that it might be too dangerous to return to my last target practice area on Exmoor, as another round of shooting there might attract the attention of a local farmer or an Exmoor ranger. This time I chose a quiet spot along the Exmoor coastline near Heddon's Mouth. I had read in a local history book that during the second world a German U Boat submarine used Heddon's Mouth as a place to sneak into at night to allow the sailors to exercise and to replenish their freshwater supplies. The place was so remote and isolated that they were able to do this without being intercepted.

To get there meant taking a two-mile footpath walk to Heddon's Mouth where a stream entered the sea across a small pebble beach. From there, I took a further half mile walk to a hidden narrow beach surrounded by trees. At this time of the year, it was very unlikely that anyone would be there.

Having partly dismantled the rifle to reduce the length, I packed it with ammunition in my backpack, some target sheets and four lengths of wood each 60 centimetres in length, a pair of binoculars and a flask of coffee and sandwiches. Suitably attired with warn clothing and weatherproofs, I set off for target practice early in the morning two days after my return from Bristol.

On reaching my destination, I found it to be as remote and abandoned as expected. I measured out a distance of 250 metres and set up four target sheets pinned to the lengths of wood, which I stuck in the sand. It was a windy day which meant that the sea was fairly rough and noisy as the waves broke approaching the shore. This was excellent for me as it would drown out the noise of the shots.

I set the rifle up resting on the tripod and fired six shots at the first target. Using the binoculars, I could see that only four bullets had hit the target sheet and these four were on the right-hand side of the sheet. I then spent an hour adjusting the sights until each shot was hitting the target with most close to the centre. I worried that the wind could be making a difference to my aim and determined to have a further test on an airless day.

Once satisfied with the sights, I concentrated on aiming for the centre of the targets. By mid-afternoon, I was getting within two inches of the centre with almost every shot. I practised shooting at the four target sheets in quick succession and could do this successfully. Using my last sheet and aiming very carefully, I hit the centre circle on the sheet twelve times out of twelve. I felt that I had made great progress.

I remained undisturbed all day except for seeing a red deer stag who came out of the woods to see what was going on. Clearly, he had never been shot at. Perhaps he was deaf, but this was unlikely. Or had he been spooked by walkers! It was clearly time to leave.

Before leaving I collected all the bullet casings, the remains of the target sheets and the sticks. As far as I could see, I left the place as I had found it with no evidence that I had ever been there.

On the journey back I met two walkers on the path from Heddon's Mouth and thankfully apart from a quick hello they took no notice of me whatsoever. Maybe they had spooked the stag I had spotted earlier!

The new shooting range area seemed to be much safer than the one in the middle of Exmoor.

Two days later, the weather changed as the day dawned with the fields all frosted over and no wind, not even a light breeze. The lack of wind would mean that the noise from shots would travel further and would probably encourage more walkers, but I decided to take a chance on this as I needed a still day to properly test the accuracy of the rifle. Equipped similarly to the previous day I made my way early in the day to the same stretch of beach near Heddon's Mouth. I re-assembled the rifle and took a few shots. Bullseye each time. This was great as it meant that the wind on the previous practice day, and the dissembling and reassembling, had not affected the sighting and it was set perfectly for my eye. I practiced shooting from different positions, standing, kneeling, lying and without the support of the tripod. I was becoming quite a marksman. After a few hours I felt ready to start my vigil in Bristol.

Chapter 32

On the following Monday I drove to Bristol and installed myself in the flat. I had purchased provisions on route and was geared up to spend a few days in the flat. I put on vinyl gloves and planned to wear them throughout my stay as I had to make sure that no fingerprints were left in the flat as the police would certainly identify where a shot had been fired from.

I set up the tripod and rifle two metres back from the bay window overlooking the supermarket entrance. Keeping the window closed, I made myself comfortable in front of the bay window and, using the binoculars, I could clearly see people entering and leaving the supermarket.

I realised that my hope that sooner or later I would see and identify a group of shoplifters was very optimistic, and that I might spend a month watching the supermarket with no positive result. I felt that it was worth taking the gamble on this and determined to make my stay as comfortable as possible. With a TV and Radio placed close to my chair and a few good books to read, I could keep boredom at bay but keep a continuous watch on the store at the same time. If after a month I did not identify shoplifters at the supermarket, then I would abandon the operation and find another way.

It would have been much easier to research a prolific shoplifter, and to target him or her, but I felt that to kill a shoplifter in the act of shoplifting would have much greater impact on the public and particularly on other shoplifters.

I stayed in the flat from Monday to Friday that week and watched the store from 9am to 9pm each day. Nothing suspicious. Got home on Friday evening at 11pm and had a relaxing weekend including a long walk each day.

The following week, the pattern was the same. Long days of watching and waiting. Nothing suspicious.

Halfway through the third week, at four in the afternoon, I noticed a group of four young adults talking together near the supermarket. One had a pram, and one had a shopping trolley on wheels. This was suspicious as shopping trolleys were generally used only by older people in this particular store and there was something about the way they behaved that drew my attention.

It was three men and a woman all in their teens or early twenties. The woman with the pram was aged about eighteen and was dressed in a hooded jacket, denim jeans and trainers. During their chat outside the supermarket, she paid no attention to the pram, which made me wonder if there was a baby inside it. The man with the trolley was in his early twenties and was similarly dressed in a hooded jacket. The other two men were shabbily dressed but again each wore a hooded jacket.

Three of them entered the store separately about five seconds apart and I noticed that each pulled up their hoods as they entered. The third man walked quickly away from the store. I felt that this could be a group of shoplifters. I opened the bay window and took up position behind the tripod and lifted the rifle into place and cocked it ready to fire. I continued to watch the entrance through binoculars and after about five minutes I heard an alarm continuously ringing from the direction of the store. People started to come out without shopping bags and a store worker started to assemble them near the front. Then the woman with the pram came out pushing a heavy load and was followed by a store manager or security man in uniform who tried to get her to stop. He was then set upon by one of her male companions who wrestled him to the ground to enable the woman with the pram to get away. She moved towards a white van, which had just pulled in near the shop entrance. Then the last man came out of the store, pushing a trolley which was heavily laden with goods, and made his way to the van. I lost sight of the man who had taken down the store manager and did not see him again.

This was all happening very fast, but I was absolutely sure that these were shoplifters. I put down the glasses and raised the rifle to the tripod. Looking through the rifle sight was similar to looking through a telescope and gave me as good a view as through the binoculars. I sighted the woman with the pram as she reached the back of the van. The man with the loaded trolley appeared beside her and opened the back of the van.

I took careful aim and fired at the woman's head. There was a spurt of blood, and she went down. I then moved the sight to the man who was frozen in shock as he looked down on the woman. My second shot hit him on the top of his head, and he fell against the van and slid down to the ground. Neither of them moved so I did not feel any need to hit them again. I moved the sighting of the rifle towards the front of the van and to my surprise the driver had opened the door and was getting out to investigate what had happened. As he was moving, I aimed at his chest and fired. He went down and I watched him for a few seconds. There was no further movement from him. I put down the rifle and looked through the binoculars. The people outside the shop were running for their lives and within a few seconds the place was deserted. I did not spot the second man, who had assaulted the store manager, so guessed that he had made his getaway when he saw what had happened. He is unlikely to go shoplifting again for a while.

I closed the window and disassembled the rifle. Once this was done, I quickly packed all my things away and prepared to leave. When packed, I went around the flat to make sure nothing was left behind. My car was parked just a few doors down from the flat and I was able to quickly take my belongings and put them in the boot. I went back to get the airbed and sleeping bag as I was concerned that the police would trace where they were purchased and that this could lead them to me. Another concern was that I might have left my DNA on either item. To deflate the airbed quickly I used a kitchen knife to cut it open and I could then roll it into an armful. Less than ten minutes after the shootings, I locked the flat for the last time, got into my car and drove down the side road leading away from Gloucester Road. I could hear sirens behind me as the police were arriving at the scene.

I avoided the M5 and the Link Road and made my way home across Somerset and Exmoor. Once I reached the relative safety of Exmoor I pulled the car into a lay-by, got out of the car and vomited the contents of my stomach. Sat back into the car and found myself shaking and trembling uncontrollably. It was the first time this had happened to me after a shooting, and it concerned me. I felt no guilt or remorse at what I had done, nor did I feel any fear. This physical reaction must have been caused by shock even though the whole act had been premeditated. Must be getting old!

Anyway, after about twenty minutes, I calmed down and felt OK to continue the journey. After another half-hour's driving, I stopped again and had coffee and sandwiches, which made me feel whole again. I determined to get control of my emotions and to make sure that I took all the necessary precautions when home to leave no clues for the police if they should visit. Rather than wait until the following day to burn the sleeping bag and airbed I decided to dump them. I remembered that in one of our neighbouring villages there was a 'green' disposal facility next to their village hall with five skips for glass, cardboard, clothing, wood and metal. I made a detour to this facility and offloaded the sleeping bag, airbed and pump, bullet casings and the wig and glasses. I also dumped the disposable gloves that I had used in Bristol and the books that I had in the Bristol flat in case the agent had seen them and could remember them. Finally, I dumped the radio I had been using. After this task I drove home.

Before going to bed, I wrapped the rifle and ammunition in a plastic bag and buried it in the garden at a depth of about 30 centimetres. I carefully raked over the vegetable bed to remove any sign of this activity including my muddy footprints. Went to bed and slept soundly until 10am.

The following morning, I dug up the rifle package and replaced it in its normal place in the old barn.

Chapter 33

The Bristol murders made national news. Initially, it was reported as a drive-by killing of three Bristol shoppers, a husband and wife and a neighbour. But once the media had a chance to speak to eyewitnesses, it changed to 'three shoplifters gunned down'. The eyewitnesses were all clear that the victims had been involved in a group shoplifting spree, which was confirmed by the supermarket manager.

At mid-day on the day after the shooting, the police gave a press conference which was broadcast on live TV. They announced that the three people killed had apparently been on an organised shoplifting activity, that only three shots had been fired in quick succession with each being a fatal shot, two in the head and one in the chest. They were still investigating exactly where the shots were fired from, and they were appealing for any witnesses at or near the scene to come forward and say what they heard or saw.

The police called a second press conference, again broadcast live on TV, to announce that they had established that the shooting had taken place from the first-floor window in a flat on Greystones Road off Gloucester Road adjacent to the supermarket. The flat had been rented for a month by a middle-aged woman who had given the letting agent a false name and address. The weapon used was believed to have been a Heckler and Koch designed SA80 rifle as used by the British army. The distance from the window to the front of the supermarket was approximately 200 metres and the fact that only three bullets were fired in quick succession, and each had been a fatal shot would indicate that the killer was a trained marksman. All local residents were being interviewed and the police were appealing to anyone who had seen either a woman or a man entering or leaving number 57 Greystones Road in the past three weeks to contact them. They went on to say there was a possibility that these killings were linked to other killings and that their investigations would fully explore this possibility.

This set the UK media into a frenzy. The newspapers quickly speculated that the killings were being carried out by a right-wing vigilante group and correctly listed the killings which might be linked, with the exception of the Irish killing which was not mentioned. However, they also listed a further seven killings as being possibly linked. I had never even heard or read about these crimes.

A few days later, the police made public the fact that the bullets in the Bristol killings had been fired from the same rifle as had been used in the Southampton killing. They also made public that forensics had identified and confirmed that the bullets used in the Taunton, Cheltenham, and Ipswich murders had been fired from the same pistol. A hallmark of each of these crimes was that each of the victims were involved in either crime or protest movements. The police invited the public to assist them by tipping them off on any suspicions they might have about a neighbour, colleague or relative.

The Bristol killings had an immediate effect on shoplifting nationwide. Organised shoplifting sprees stopped immediately, and it was several months before any similar raid was reported. Shoplifting by individuals decreased nationally by over 80% for the following three months and shopkeepers and staff felt safer at work than they had felt for years. Several newspaper articles and TV programmes presented this as clear evidence that the way to deal with shoplifting in the longer term was to arrest and imprison them.

Chapter 34

I watched with great interest as the story developed. Strangely, I felt detached from the story as if I did not belong within it. As public interest grew in the case and the police gradually built up a picture, I should have felt scared and vulnerable but instead I felt calm and comfortable within myself. I had no regrets about anything I had done and actually felt that I had performed a public service. This was echoed by some newspapers who said that the vigilantes had highlighted how the government had failed to deal adequately with criminals and disruptive protestors and that it was no surprise that some group had taken the law into their own hands.

I knew that if the police did identify and arrest me it would be very embarrassing for my children and grandchildren. This could not be helped, and I had already decided that I would not apologise to them for what I had done but only for the distress my actions had caused them.

Gradually, the police moved towards deciding that the culprit was a middle-aged woman. However, it appeared that they had no real lead as to who this woman was. I was worried that a connection with the Irish case would be established as I had left more clues about myself there, than at any of the other crime scenes,

It was time to change my car as it could easily become established that the killer drove a silver BMW. I could not hide the fact that I had owned such a car, and changed it, but at least by not having the car when the police arrived could work in my favour. I drove to Exeter and visited the BMW dealer my husband had always used. I explained that I wanted to change to a smaller car as my annual mileage was low and I rarely left North Devon. Their advice was for me to have a BMW 2 Series Active Tourer Electric. I did not want an Electric car due to the continuing shortage of charging points, so I settled for a petrol driven variant. They had a red model in stock, so I was able to trade-in my old car and have the new one straight away. As my husband had dealt with this dealer for many years, there was nothing unusual about me changing my car. It looked good on my drive and the neighbours would soon forget that I used to have a silver car.

On Thursday evening, my vigilante activities featured as a discussion on Question Time on BBC1. The panel of five were all politically correct and condemned the vigilante as a serial killer acting as judge jury and executioner.

Members of the audience however were more willing to step outside the box and several speakers applauded my activities. One said that if and when caught, I should be given a medal as big as a frying pan. Another pointed out the vigilante had single-handedly reduced organised shoplifting in recent days by 90% and had virtually stopped all disruptive behaviour of the 'Just Stop Oil' protesters, who now continued to protest but without disrupting the lives of members of the public. Their tactics changed to defacing works of art in galleries and public places like Stonehenge. This was still very annoying to the public but did not interrupt their lives. Another member of the audience speculated that criminals and anti-social groups now feared the vigilante more than the police.

The panel members conceded that the vigilante had highlighted the fact that anti-social activity such as shoplifting and disruption were left uncontrolled by the police as the Crime Prosecution Service were reluctant to take such crimes to court, and those that did go to court got very mild punishment. They also conceded that the vigilante killings were having a huge deterrent effect on these activities. However, the vigilante was himself or herself lawless and a criminal who needed to be caught and punished as otherwise there could be copycat killings and society could descend into anarchy.

I could not agree with the latter premise as I firmly believed that others would not copy my actions through fear of being caught and punished with years in prison. For me such fear was minimal as I was 75 years old and the prospect of spending my last few years in prison did not unduly worry me. At least I would be fed and well looked-after.

I had been a good citizen for most of my life, and my recent criminal activities had made a valuable contribution to society.

Chapter 35

Simon Cooper had become increasingly concerned about his mother in Devon. Over the past two years, he had noticed a change in her lifestyle whereby she was often not at home, and she was reticent about telling him where she had been. Often when he telephoned her, there was no answer. As the police and the media moved towards blaming a middle-aged or elderly woman for the spate of killings, he began to worry that the culprit could be his mother. He knew that she had a rifle and a pistol in the house, which had both belonged to his late father. Both he and his sister had, many years ago, discovered the loose floorboards in the bedroom under which was stored the guns and a large quantity of ammunition. Neither of them had ever told their parents that they had found this hideout and knew that these arms existed.

When he read in the papers about the gangster killing in Ireland, he realised that it was in the same week that his Mother was not answering her phone for several days and when she eventually telephoned him to return his calls she said that she had been away for a few days break and had forgotten to take her mobile phone with her.

Simon decided that it was time to tackle this head-on with her to establish if his fears were justified. He asked his mother if he could come down to Devon to see her as he had something he needed to discuss. He considered discussing this with his sister Anne in Australia but decided against doing so as it would alarm and distress her.

He drove to Devon to see his mother on 7th December. After a delicious meal she had prepared for them both, he told her of his concerns,

As expected, she denied having anything to do with any of the murders. He then told her that he knew about the guns hidden under the floorboards in the main bedroom. She laughed at this and said that his father had got rid of the guns and ammunition some months before he died. As far as she knew, he had given them back to the army. She knew that he would want to check this so invited him to go to her bedroom and examine the place with the loose floorboards. Having let him see and examine the empty recess under the floorboards, she then invited him to examine the contents of the safe which he knew was kept in a cupboard in the study. She satisfied him that this was also arms free.

She invited him to search the house, but he declined this saying that if she still had them, they would have been under the floorboards.

He then asked her about all the trips away from home that she was making. She explained that being in the house on her own sometimes caused her claustrophobia and she needed to get away now and then. She often did not tell him of her planned trips as she felt sure that he would invite her to visit him instead, and she did not want to become a nuisance to him and his family. She enjoyed going to different places in the UK and staying in hotels and hoped he would not mind if she continued to do so.

After lengthy conversations throughout the next day, he was reasonably satisfied that she was telling the truth but still had a niggling doubt. He knew that his mother had right wing views and knew that each of the people killed would have been seen by her as useless human beings. He was also surprised that she had not taken any offence at his accusations.

He decided that he would keep close tabs on her from then on and try to establish from her in advance of each trip where she was going.

Chapter 36

On Tuesday 9th January, I had an appointment to have my hair styled and coloured. I arrived at my favourite salon in Barnstaple at 11am and was looking forward to two hours relaxation being pampered and chatting to my stylist and the staff in the salon.

I had completed having my hair washed and was ready to have colour foils applied when suddenly a man aged about thirty entered the salon and walked through to the centre of the long room. He was a white man, about five foot eight inches tall, of slim build and had long black hair. He was dressed in combat style trousers, boots and a zipped jacket with front and side pockets. He produced a pistol from inside his jacket and started shooting at customers and staff. The place immediately went into a state of shock and panic with people screaming and diving for cover. There were nineteen people in the salon with three more upstairs. In just a few seconds he had shot five people. It all happened so fast. People were screaming in pain or fear, and I saw that at least two were not moving. He stood in the middle of the salon with his back to me. In a split second I remembered that a terrorist on a train in France or Germany had started shooting passengers in a carriage and was only prevented from killing everyone by one passenger attacking him and knocking him down. Other passengers had then joined in, and he was disarmed and overcome. I decided that this gunman must be stopped, or he would kill us all. I picked up a stylist's scissors ran towards him as fast as I could and stabbed him hard in the neck with the scissors. He fired a shot at me but missed. I kept hold of the scissors and the momentum of my run pushed us both against a stylist's cabinet. As he fell, with me falling with him, he knocked over the stylist's cabinet which stood a metre high and had a sharp corner. He hit the cabinet sideways on with such force that it broke away from its fixings and would have hurt his ribs severely. He then struck his head against a mirror on the wall, breaking the glass, but somehow the glass remained intact within the mirror. He ended up in a heap lying across the cabinet which was now on its side. I had fallen with him, but he cushioned my fall, and I ended up on top of him with just a searing pain in my upper arm. I let go of the scissors, which were embedded in his neck, groped for his face with my hand and poked my two forefingers into his eyes with the palm of my hand on his nose. My manicured nails were quite long and sharp and as I dug into his eyes, I could feel my nails cutting flesh. He screamed and got one of his hands up to his eyes, with the other hand going to his neck. The gun was no longer in his hand, but I could not see it. As I lay on top of him, I realised that one of my legs was between his. I proceeded to knee him as hard as I could in the groin several times. I knew that this would disable him for a minute or two. All of the above took place in a matter of three or four seconds.

I rolled off the man and found the pistol on the floor. He was still holding both hands to his eyes and neck and groaning in agony. At this point, I saw that blood was running down my arm and realized that I had been shot. I dragged myself away from him. At my age, I find it difficult to get back on my feet from a lying position but with the help of a stylist's chair to lean on and an adrenaline rush, I quickly got back on my feet. I was about two metres from the man who was now groaning and wriggling on the ground. I held the pistol in my left hand, aimed at his head and shot him. He fell back and lay still as blood gushed from his forehead. I turned towards the front door in case he had an accomplice but there was no sign of another gunman and the street outside was quiet.

I put the gun down on a stylist's cabinet and sat down. My arm was now paining me badly and blood was flowing from it. The salon had gone very quiet from the shock of all that had happened. I asked in a loud voice if someone would phone for the police and ambulances and said that the police needed to be told that the gunman has been disarmed and disabled and that it was safe for them to come to the salon. I then asked if those who had not been injured would tend to the wounded and reassure them that help was on its way. I then started to tremble, felt a release of tension and burst into tears. I surprised myself at this reaction, and quickly pulling myself together pulled off my jumper to examine my wound. A stylist named Yvonne came to help me and went to get a bandage from the first aid cabinet. I tried to stem the blood and could see that the bullet had entered a fleshy part of my arm and gone through and out the other side. Both wounds were bleeding, but I was relieved that it was just a flesh wound. It had not stopped me from holding the pistol and shooting the gunman using that arm.

It took about ten minutes until the police arrived and by the time the ambulance crew arrived, the police had established that three people had died and a further three had been shot and injured. Another elderly woman had fallen during the panic and cut her had badly against a step.

In addition, the gunman was dead. Of the five injured, two were seriously hurt and three had relatively minor injuries. One of the dead was a staff member and two were customers. Two of the injured were staff members and three including myself were customers. All eight victims were female ranging in age from 19 to 75.

I sat quietly while the police dealt with the aftermath, established what had happened, and got the injured away to hospital. As my bleeding had now stopped, I asked the police and ambulance crew if I could delay going to hospital until after the police had taken statements including mine. This was agreed and the police then took statements from all the witnesses to the shootings. They took a brief statement from me. Whilst this was going on, all witnesses were asked to stay in the salon, which took about two hours. The four dead were left where they lay but the police covered them over with sheets. Once all the statements had been taken, the staff and customers were allowed to go home, and it was agreed that I needed to go to hospital. The police asked if an officer could accompany me in the ambulance which I agreed. A group of forensic police then entered the salon to begin their crime scene work. I was taken out the rear entrance and went into a waiting ambulance.

The police officer, who was an inspector, explained to me that as I had participated in the shootings and had actually killed someone, they would have to stay with me in the hospital. If the hospital doctor felt that

I needed to stay in the hospital overnight, the police would need to question me in more detail about the event. If released from the hospital, they would need to take me to the police station for further questioning. I asked if this meant that I was being arrested for killing the gunman. The inspector said that I was not being arrested or charged with anything but because I had killed a person, they would need to hold me for some time until they had completed their enquiries and had questioned me fully about the incident.

After arriving in the Accident and Emergency ward at the hospital, I was immediately seen by two doctors who examined my injured arm. They said I would need an Xray to make sure there was no metal left in the wound, and that they would then clean the wound and stitch it. This process took about twenty minutes. The doctors satisfied themselves that I had no other injuries and released me. They said I should get an early night as I may be suffering from shock.

The police asked if I felt well enough and was willing to accompany them to the station. I agreed and went with them in a police car, using a side exit from the hospital to avoid a group of media people, who were apparently gathered at the hospital entrance.

The police were kind and courteous throughout the interrogation process. I was given tea and sandwiches on arrival at the station. When I expressed concern about being fined because my parking ticket had expired, they assured me that an officer would get this sorted with the local council and ensure that I would not be fined. They offered to pick up the car and drive it to my home, so I gave them my car keys and address. They said that they would drive me home.

The interrogation itself was thorough. Having heard all the other witness statements, my interrogators knew that what I had done was in self-defence and in defence of others. Their main concern was that the gunman had already been disabled when I shot him and that instead of shooting him, I should have held him at gunpoint until the police arrived. My defence to this was that he had already identified himself as a mass killer, that the injury to his eyes, neck and testicles were temporary and relatively minor and that I had to shoot him before he recovered his composure in order to prevent him from killing more. I did not have the confidence that I would be able to hold him at bay if he recovered before the police arrived.

I admitted that I was angry when I shot him but denied having lost my temper. I also admitted that I was afraid of him. They then wanted to know how I had learnt to shoot so well. The bullet I fired from two or three metres away had struck the centre of his forehead which was effectively a bullseye. I assured them that I had never fired a pistol before and that having aimed at his forehead from such close range I was not surprised that this was where he was hit. The fact that my shot had killed him was down to luck rather than judgement. They then wanted to know where I had learnt to tackle a man younger, larger and heavier than me and to successfully disable him within a few seconds. I said that the situation had inspired and driven me to make a superhuman effort to save myself and others. The police appeared to be sceptical about this response.

They asked countless questions about my background, my career, my late husband and my children.

The Inspector who had accompanied me to the hospital eventually explained that as the law stood, because I had shot and killed a man apparently, but not necessarily, in self-defence, they would have to charge me with manslaughter. He assured me that this charge could be overturned by a court. Justice would then be seen to have been done by having a court establish and rule that I was guilty of no crime. I felt that this all seemed a bit pathetic but was anxious to be compliant with the police so that they would continue to see me as a rather simple, but tough, innocent old lady, who had acted instinctively to help people. The police said they would charge me immediately and then release me on a peppercorn bail of one pound and allow me to go home. This formal process took about fifteen minutes, and I was then released and told that I was free to go.

The police then told me that the afternoon's events had become a huge news story and that there were TV camera crews and newspaper reporters waiting outside the station hoping to see me and interview me as I left the station. They asked if I would prefer to leave the station from a rear exit and be driven home in a police car or if I was prepared to meet the press. I said that I was exhausted after the day's events and would just like to go home.

They said that the media people would be relentless in pursuing me for a statement and suggested that I should agree to meet them the following morning and answer their questions to which I agreed.

The police then took me to a rear exit, into a car and drove me home.

There were a group of media people outside my drive. The police said they would get me into the house and would then explain to the press that I would speak to them in the morning.

The police said that they would attend in the morning to ensure that the media people behaved properly with me.

Chapter 37

The first thing I did when home was to make telephone calls to both my daughter in Australia, my son in Lancashire and my friend Tom to assure them that I was O K. I did facetime calls, and I could see that they were relieved to see me in good shape. They each knew what had happened and Anne and Simon had been speaking to one another earlier. I also spoke to my three grandchildren who each said that they now had a Supergran and that they were proud of what I had done. I warned both Anne and Simon not to get too excited about my heroism as the police had charged me with manslaughter for killing the gunman while he was disarmed and disabled. They were both shocked at this and said that the public would not stand for it. They both seemed to know everything that happened in great detail. Anne was able to tell me that what had happened in Barnstaple was headline news in Australia and that I was being hailed as a hero throughout the world. The calls took about an hour and when they were finished, I was able to sit down and think for the first time since the shooting.

Having spent the last year working so hard to maintain a low profile and remain anonymous, I had now inadvertently thrust myself into the limelight. This was very dangerous indeed. Every adult throughout the United Kingdom and Ireland were going to see my photograph in the papers and my image on TV, with the probability that someone would recognise me from having been at or near the scene of one of my killings. Luckily my face and hair had been disguised at some of them, but not at all of them.

I realised that it would be impossible to avoid contact with the press and that it was better to see them and get it all over with as quickly as possible.

I was particularly vulnerable from the Irish trip as I was seen by several people there including the bodyguard of Adrian Reilly. Although I had been wearing a blond wig and glasses during our encounter, he had seen me up close and he had effectively witnessed the murder.

I must prepare myself for a less than friendly visit from the police.

After preparing and eating bacon, eggs and chips I settled down to watch the 'news at ten'. The events in Barnstaple dominated the news and it felt surreal watching people I knew giving interviews and talking about me on TV. The news included details of a police press conference during which they explained that following their investigation of what happened and their interviews with witnesses including with me, and taking into account that the gunman had already been disabled when I shot him, they had charged me with manslaughter as my shooting him was not in self-defence. They would leave it to a court to decide whether, or not, I was guilty of a crime. Because of the circumstances of the incident, they had released me on bail pending a trial.

The media reaction to this police statement was almost universal outrage. How could the police charge me with manslaughter when I had risked my life to save the lives of many people. Instead of treating me as a criminal I should be praised and rewarded for what I had done.

Because of my concerns about being identified as the vigilante killer I was unable to take any pleasure from the positive things that were being said about me. I went to bed that evening feeling depressed that my newfound fame would turn to universal revulsion within a few days.

Chapter 38

The following day was chaotic. At 8am, the doorbell chimed, and I got up and dressed quickly. Answered the door to a TV crew, who immediately started filming me at the door. I could see many more reporters in the background and when I looked around the side of the porch, I saw that there were about a hundred people on my drive. I said to the first lady at the door that I needed half an hour to have a bath, get dressed properly and have a cup of tea and that I would then step out of the house and answer questions from the group. They readily agreed to this, asked if it was OK for them to be on my drive, which I agreed, and I then closed the front door. I put on the kettle, had a quick shower, brushed my hair and dressed in a tweed suit over a black top. I changed the dressing on my arm, replacing it with a much smaller dressing, and then no sign of it could be seen under my jacket. I had a quick look at the headlines on SKY news as I drank a cup of tea. The only story running was about yesterday's events in Barnstaple. The gunman was identified as a British man who had a history of mental health problems, but who had never been convicted of a crime. I phoned one of my neighbours and asked if she would buy all of today's newspapers for me as I was unable to leave the house.

When I stepped out into the yard, the media group had prepared a platform similar to a table and asked would I mind standing on this as then they could all see me. They had obviously agreed an orderly way to ask questions with the BBC leading the way.

"Good morning, Mrs Cooper. We hope that you are feeling well today and that you have had a good night's sleep. How do you feel about the police charging you with manslaughter"?

I replied: "Thank you, I am feeling very well this morning although somewhat tired as I did not sleep very well. My injury, I said, tapping my left arm, is healing up nicely. I was surprised at the police charging me as I did not feel that I had done wrong in shooting the gunman. He had already killed and injured some of us, so he had to be stopped. However, I can understand why the police took this action. They have to act according to the law, and clearly, I had killed a man, and in their view, once the man had been disarmed and disabled, I was no longer acting in self-defence. The police have told me that a court would decide whether it was self-defence or not, having taken into account all that was happening and the situation I had found myself in.

Before the next question may I ask how the injured people are doing?"

SKY News was next: "We understand that all of the injured have improved overnight and none remain critically injured at this time. People are wondering what has happened to you in the past to make you act so fearlessly and courageously in yesterday's crisis?"

I replied: “I was neither courageous nor fearless. Actually, I was very afraid when the gunman started shooting and felt that I was about to die. My memory reverted back to a terrorist incident some years ago on a continental train when a terrorist was foiled by the quick action of a passenger who attacked the man and then with the help of others disarmed him. I also realised that this man would kill us all if he was not stopped. At my age, the fear of death is minimal as I will be facing death soon anyway, so I had nothing to lose by having a go at stopping him.”

The telegraph was next: ‘If you could re-live yesterday’s attack would you do anything differently? ‘

I replied: “I regret that I did not act more quickly than I did. If I had acted two seconds earlier, it could have saved a few others from being shot. Apart from that, I would not have done anything differently. I have no regrets about what I did and if I am now to be found guilty of a crime then so be it. In my mind, I have committed no crime."

The Sun was next: "You killed the gunman with one shot using his gun. Have you ever shot a pistol before and how did you feel when you realized that you had killed him?"

I replied: "I have never held or fired a gun before in my life. When I pulled the trigger, the gun recoiled in my hand, and I nearly dropped it. I was so close to the gunman that it would have been hard to miss him. When I shot and hit him, my immediate feeling was relief. I still feel relieved that he is dead."

ITV.: "How do your children feel about what you did?"

My response: "I spoke to my daughter in Australia and my son in Lancashire last night and also to my three grandchildren. They were surprised but pleased with what I did and glad that I escaped with just a minor injury. Both Paul and Anne felt that it was outrageous that I have been charged with manslaughter."

Daily Mail: "You will be recognised as a hero wherever you go from now on. How will you feel about this? "

My response: "I do not feel like a hero. What I did yesterday could have been done by anyone. I just happened to be in the right place at the right time and was the first to react. I was lucky to succeed in disarming him. It could easily have gone the other way, and he certainly would have killed me had he been able to keep the gun. At the end of the day, I was simply trying to save my own skin, and the bonus was that I saved a few others in the process. Hopefully, this will all be forgotten in a week's time,"

The Mirror: "It has emerged that the gunman was married and had two children. What do you have to say to them? '

My response: 'I express my deepest sympathy to them. His wife and children will mourn their loved one, but unfortunately, he had some sort of mental breakdown and became a threat to society and had to be stopped. I hope that they do not suffer criticism for what he did as only he was responsible for his actions'.

Sky News: 'Your quick action of stabbing him with a scissors followed by stabbing him in the eyes with your fingers would indicate that you have some experience in face-to-face combat. Have you done something similar in your past?'

My Response: 'No, I have never tackled a man before like this. I read crime thrillers and probably learnt something from them. My actions were instinctive self-preservation actions, aimed to stop a brutal situation.'

Daily Telegraph: 'You seem remarkably calm after such a catastrophic experience. How did you learn to take such traumatic experiences in your stride?'

My Response: 'I know that what I did yesterday seems very dramatic to you. But to me, I simply reacted to a situation, was successful in stopping the gunman and killed him. I may have appeared calm but inwardly I was quaking. The police think that I should not have shot the gunman once he was disabled and I had his gun but although I had temporarily disabled him, he was a young strong man and I was conscious of my age and physical limitations and was afraid that once he recovered, I would not be able to contain him, so I shot him'

The Sun: 'But apart from being afraid of him, you must have felt anger towards him? '

My Response: 'Yes, of course I felt anger towards him. He had shot a number of people I knew and was intent on shooting more. I was relieved when I realised that he was dead.'

At that stage two police officers arrived on the drive and interrupted proceedings to say that they needed to see me alone in the house. I thanked the media group and led the police officers into the house.

I offered them tea which they declined and said that they had good news for me. We sat in the lounge and the senior officer, who was an Inspector told me that thanks to an intervention by the Home Secretary the charges against me were dropped and that I had not committed any crime. On reviewing the investigations, it had now been determined and agreed that my actions were purely in self-defence. The police would be announcing this at a press conference later this morning.

He then asked if I was taking telephone calls. I said that the phone had already rang a few times this morning but that I had been too busy to answer it. He said that the Prime Minister was anxious to speak to me and that 10 Downing Street had asked the police to see if I would take his call. I said that of course I would speak to him. The Inspector then made arrangements using his radio and within a few minutes the phone rang. The police had offered to leave while I took the call, but I asked them to stay.

I answered the phone, and the female caller introduced herself as the Prime

Minister's Office at 10 Downing Street and asked if I would speak to the Prime Minister. Then the PM himself came on the line. He was calling to thank me on behalf of the nation for my quick thinking and bravery in tackling the gunman and for saving so many lives. He asked about my injury and how I was coping with all the media attention. He had just watched my press conference on TV and complemented me on my poise and elegance. I was surprised at how quickly he put me at ease, and we chatted for a few minutes. He apologised that I had been charged by the police and was glad that the charge had now been dropped. I thanked him for arranging this and he just laughed. He wished me well for the future and thanked me for talking to him. He hoped to meet me at some time in the future. I said that it was a pleasure and an honour to receive his call.

When I hung up, the two police officers clapped and said that I had done brilliantly. They asked if I felt comfortable being left alone to deal with the media and gave me a telephone number to use if I needed their help at any time. As they were leaving, the Inspector suggested that I might like to watch Prime Minister's Questions at midday. The Inspector spoke to the media group presumably to say there would be a press conference and within two minutes all the group were gone, and I was left alone again.

I read the papers for the rest of the morning and then watched PMQs. In his opening remarks the PM said that he was sure that the whole house would share his horror at the shooting incident in Barnstaple, in Devon, and share his sympathy and condolences to the injured and the families of those who had died. He had spoken on the telephone to Lorna Cooper, the lady who had so bravely tackled the gunman, and thanked her on behalf of the nation for her amazing action which had saved so many lives. The Home Secretary, after reviewing the case, had ordered that the charges against Lorna Cooper be dropped as the nation owed her a debt of gratitude and her actions had not been unlawful. The PM's sentiments were fully supported by the Leader of the Opposition and by the leaders of the other parties in the house.

I thought to myself that I had now got myself into a fine mess. When my inevitable unmasking as the vigilante took place, it would now be a hundred times more dramatic than it would have been without yesterday's events.

Chapter 39

Following a week of intense media interest after the Barnstaple incident during which I was invited to appear on several TV programmes but declined, things began to quieten down and life was returning to normal.

I felt sure that it was only a matter of time until the police uncovered my identity. Too many people had seen me at the various crime locations but particularly in Ireland. I had to consider how I would deal with the police if they came and claimed that I had been seen at or near the scene of one or more of the killings on the relevant date or dates.

Stout denial was usually a good defence when a witness was unsure and would probably be a safe approach to take for the killing in Taunton, as I had not had my car there on the day of the killing and I had not stayed in the town overnight.

I could also deny having been in Cheltenham on the day of that killing. I had parked my car several miles from the location of the crime and had been careful to avoid motorway and link road cameras on my routes there and back. Also, it was over a year since then, and it was very unlikely that any security footage would still exist.

On reviewing my Southampton activities, I decided that it would be safe to deny having been there also. I had my face disguised when near the crime scene and my car had been parked in a suburb well away from the scene. Also, it was a year since the crime and highly unlikely that any CCTV footage would still exist.

Ipswich was more worrying. Although I had not taken my car there, I had stayed in two hotels and dined in two restaurants so it was certainly possible that any staff might remember me. I had used my own name and address in the hotels so there would be records of my stays. If the police asked me if I had been to Ipswich, I would have to deny that I had been there. If they then produced evidence that I had been there, I would admit that I had been there on a pleasure trip and say that the reason I had denied it was because my children had not known about some of my short holidays away and would worry about me travelling such long distances alone. They might then establish the dates, which would look incriminating.

I next considered my time in Bristol. I had been seen and had discussions with the Estate Agent for the flat and although disguised with glasses and a wig, he might identify me from my media appearances. I had also been seen by a few people as I entered and left the flat on occasions. However, on balance it was unlikely that any of these could make a positive ID. I had been careful to avoid routes that would have CCTV cameras. But there was a risk.

The crime which left me most vulnerable and was likely to be my downfall was the killing in Ireland. I had taken my car there, booked it onto two ferry trips and I had been stopped by police on the evening of the crime. I had been seen by many people on the ferries, in hotels and restaurants and I had even been seen at close quarters by the police officer guarding the victim. If the police got any reports that I had been seen in Ireland during that week, they would be able to find evidence that I had been there and that my car had been there.

I decided that the Irish crime was the most likely one to lead the police to me.

I was annoyed with myself for being so amateurish when planning and conducting each of my crimes. Although I had accepted from the outset that I was likely to be caught and punished, I no longer felt comfortable with the prospect of being caught. I made up my mind that I would maintain my innocence with the police until they had produced enough evidence to convict me, and only then would I admit to what I had done.

In preparation for the police finding that I had been in Ireland in the week of the Drogheda killing, I decided that if confronted I would make no secret of having had a motoring holiday in Ireland during last August. I would then have to tell both of my children that I had gone to Ireland for a few days in August. It would be awkward explaining why I had not told them of this trip before now, particularly with Simon as I would have driven within a few miles of his home twice that week as I drove to the ferry-port in Scotland and returned from there a few days later. I needed to come up with a good excuse for not telling him about this trip.

I would tell them that when their father served in the army in Northern Ireland during the troubles he had told me many stories about his adventures in Ulster. I went there for a week last summer to see some of these places and had not told Simon or Anne in case they thought that I was pining for Dad and was undergoing some form of stress.

I would tell them all about the places I visited and how beautiful Northern Ireland was.

Depending on what action the police were taking, I would maintain my innocence with both the police and my children until evidence produced by the police was irrefutable.

It was clearly going to be a very difficult time.

Chapter 40 - February 2024

Early in February, the police inspector who had interviewed me after the Barnstaple gunman event, arrived at my door accompanied by a female police officer. I invited them in and offered tea which was declined.

Inspector Swaminathan inquired about my health and how I had recovered from all the events and media interest in January before getting down to the real purpose of his visit. He asked if I would mind if they recorded the rest of our conversation. I expressed surprise but said that this was OK. The female officer then placed her phone on a coffee table to record the conversation.

He explained that following my appearance on various TV bulletins and my photograph being published in all the newspapers, the police had received reports from members of the public claiming to identify me as the woman involved in a number of shootings which had taken place around the country during last year. He said that this was not unusual as people suddenly placed in the public eye were often mistaken for someone else. However, the police were obliged to investigate such reports and therefore I had become the subject of police investigations into the reports they had received. This should not cause me any undue concern as hopefully it was just a matter of the police satisfying themselves that this was mistaken identity and that I could not have been involved in the crimes he had referred to.

I expressed surprise at all of this and asked what specific crimes he was referring to. He avoided answering this directly and just said that during 2023 a number of murders had taken place around the country and that the police had reason to believe that these were carried out by a woman, and when my photo was published and appearances on TV took place relating to my shooting the Barnstaple gunman, some members of the public associated me with one of the murders and claimed to have identified me as being present at or near, the scene of one of the murders.

He explained that the first thing the police wished to do was to search my house and garden and any other property I had for any evidence of my involvement in any of the crimes. If I was willing to give my permission for such a search, it could be done immediately. If I was not prepared to agree to a search they would get a search warrant. I said that there would be no need for that as I was quite happy for them to search the house and garden as thoroughly as they required, and they could do this straight away.

Inspector Swaminathan said that the police would like to take my mobile phone and any PCs or Laptops that I had for a few days to search the data on them for any incriminating evidence. This I agreed to.

He said they would need all of my bank statements for each account that I had, and all credit card statements for each account that I had covering the last two years. I said that I had two bank accounts, a current account and a deposit account and that I did not keep paper statements for either account. However, all the statements were online, and I would be happy to give the police my IDs and passwords to access the accounts. He asked for these, and I wrote the name of the bank and the account numbers, how to access them online and the IDs and password details. I confirmed that I had no credit card accounts and had not had one since before 2018 when I had a Barclaycard. In response to a further question, I confirmed that I had no store cards, or other methods of making payments.

He said they would also like to have a lengthy formal interview with me regarding all my activities and journeys during last year. He would give me a list of dates and ask if I could remember or had any record of where I had been on those dates. If I was agreeable to accompany him to the police station today for this interview, the search of my house and garden could take place at the same time. He assured me that the police would conduct a very tidy search and that everything would be replaced as found.

I agreed to all of these, and he telephoned the station to arrange for the search team to come. They arrived in less than ten minutes, which to me, meant that they had already been organised and were waiting around the corner. Six officers, four men and two women, arrived at the door as

Inspector Swaminathan and I and the female officer left for Barnstaple in a police car. I had left my front door key, car-keys and the key for a small safe I used for storing documents. I had also left the key for the lock-up garage where the Jaguar was kept, and the Jaguar key having explained where this was located. They asked if they could examine my bank accounts, and the Inspector told them that he already had my permission to do this and he had the necessary details to access my bank account.

Inspector Swaminathan and indeed all of the other officers I met were very polite and courteous throughout and did not in any way treat me as a criminal. I concluded, and hoped, that they were not taking the claim that I was a murderer seriously and were simply going through the motions of an investigation. However, they would be thorough, and I would need to be very careful with everything I said during the interview. As the interview was less than 15 minutes away, there was little time to prepare.

Mentally, I reviewed the house and garden. There was nothing to be found. All clothing worn at each crime scene had been disposed of and replaced. The guns were safely stowed away from the house. There was nothing buried or hidden in the garden and there was nothing at the garage or in the Jaguar. If they found the space under the loose floorboards in my bedroom it was empty and had been well cleaned.

The telephone and laptop were a bit of a worry but should be OK. I had not taken my mobile with me on any missions so it could not be located at any of the crime scenes. I had not made any telephone calls in connection with any of the missions. I had not used either the phone or the laptop to google any incriminating websites or done any of my research on either of them. I had not made any bookings by phone. I could not think of anything else which might be on either device which would catch me out.

I had been careful not to use my debit card for any payments whilst out on a mission. I paid for all hotels, meals, petrol, and incidentals in cash. I even paid the rent on the Bristol flat in cash. The police would ask why I paid for so many things in cash whilst having a debit card to which I would reply that I had paid cash all my life, that I had always carried cash in my purse and would continue to do so. If concerned about the amount of cash I had withdrawn over the year, given my lifestyle, I would reluctantly admit to a gambling habit which had cost a thousand or two over the past year, during visits to the races at Taunton, Exeter, Newton Abbott and Chepstow.

When we arrived at the police station, I was taken to an interview room where Inspector Swaminathan introduced me to Detective Inspector Cartland from Scotland Yard. I jokingly said that I was honoured to be interviewed by such senior and distinguished officers. They said that as the interview was voluntary, and that I was not under caution, I did not have to have a solicitor present but that if I would like to have one then they would be happy to arrange it. I declined this offer and said that I was happy to be interviewed alone.

The D.I. did most of the talking and asked all of the questions.

D.I. Cartland: "This interview has come about because we have had reports that you were seen at or near a number of crime scenes last year. Each report is from a witness who saw you on television, or saw your photograph in newspapers last month, and felt that you closely resemble a person they saw at or near a crime scene last year. These reports have prompted us to investigate you with a view to establishing whether or not you were involved in any criminal activity last year. Other than these reports, we have no evidence that you were in any way involved, which is why we are searching your home, your car and your phone, laptop and bank accounts. We are hopeful that our searches will not uncover anything incriminating and indeed that they will provide evidence that you were not in the vicinity of the crime scenes on the dates of the crimes. We are also hopeful that during our interview you will be able to, with help from your memory and your personal records, provide alibis for the dates in question.

The crimes we are investigating and which we feel are possibly linked to one perpetrator are:

Number 1: A man named Nigel Boland was shot and killed in Taunton on 14th September 2022

Number 2: A man named Earnest Matthews was shot and killed in Cheltenham on 24th November 2022

Number 3: A man named Alan Dudley was shot and killed in Southampton on 27th December 2022

Number 4: A man named Amir Bukhari was shot and killed on 27th March 2023 in Reading

Number 5: A man named Donald Turner was shot and killed in Ipswich on 22nd July 2023

Number 6: Three people were shot and killed in Bristol on 1st November 2023 outside a supermarket. They were Anne Torsney, Peter Torsney and Francis Maher.

Witnesses have claimed to have seen you in Southampton during December 2022, in Ipswich on July 24th and 25th

2023 and in Bristol during November 2023.

Let us start with Taunton. Were you in Taunton at any time during September 2022? "

I replied: "You are asking me to remember what I did throughout September the year before last. I cannot recall this immediately. Exeter and Taunton are the two nearest cities to my home. I travel to both regularly for shopping, eating and other leisure activities. I may have been to Taunton during September two years ago, but I cannot give you a date."

D.I. Cartland: "I will ask if you have visited the other locations during the past two years. We will then get down to times and dates.

Have you been to Cheltenham in the past two years?"

I replied: "No. I have not been to Cheltenham for over five years. I used to go to attend race meetings there with my husband, who died in 2019."

D.I. Cartland: "Right. Have you been to Southampton in the past two years?"

I replied: "No. I have not been there for at least ten years."

D.I. Cartland: "Have you been in Reading in the past year?".

I replied: "No, I have not been in Reading in the past year. Except to pass through it on the train to London a few times."

D.I. Cartland: "Have you been to Ipswich during last year?",

I replied: “It is several years since I have been to Ipswich.”

D.I. Cartland: “Have you been to Bristol during the last six months?”

I Replied: “Yes. I go to Bristol two or three times a year for shopping, to go to the theatre, and I occasionally stay in a hotel overnight. “

D.I. Cartland: “Right. We will come back to Bristol in a minute. You say that you have not visited Cheltenham, Southampton, or Ipswich during the past two years. Is that correct?”.

I replied: “Yes, that is correct.”

D.I. Cartland: “Do you keep a diary, or do you keep receipts from shopping, meals and personal items? “

I replied: “No, I do not keep a diary. Never have. I keep certain receipts for a while in case I need to return something but then I throw them out. Your officers will find any receipts I have kept but I doubt if any will go back a year and a half."

D.I. Cartland: "Do you pay most of your bills using your debit card?"

I replied: "I pay many of my bills using my online bank account and pay by BACS (Bank Automated Credit System). I pay most of my external payments in cash. I obtain this cash by using 'hole in the wall' cash machines with my debit card."

The interrogation went on for a further two hours. I felt that I had satisfied him that I had not been in the vicinity of the crimes on the dates mentioned although I could not provide definitive proof. I also felt reasonably confident that any witnesses would not be able to swear that I was the person they saw. The police could of course ask all the hotels in each city if I had stayed with them on or near the relevant dates, but it was probably unlikely that they would investigate in such detail unless one of the witnesses was an employee in one of the hotels, I had stayed in.

There were still many dangers to worry about.

My biggest concern however was what happened in Ireland. The police had not mentioned this crime so far, but I felt sure that they would have this crime linked to those they had already mentioned. I decided that when they did come on to Ireland, I would admit to having been in Northern Ireland on a motoring holiday during the previous summer. This would explain why witnesses may have seen me in the various places I had visited (hopefully excepting Drogheda). I was also conscious that they could establish from the ferry company that my car and I had travelled on their ferry.

As the interview drew to a close, I realised that they were not going to mention Ireland at this stage in their investigation.

The D.I. advised me that they may want to interview me again when they had completed the search of my property, the telephone and the laptop. I was driven home in an unmarked police car.

A week later, I had a visit from two police officers who returned my telephone and laptop. They confirmed that they had found nothing incriminating on either device or within my home, car or garden and that they were confident that D.I Cartland would let me know soon that they had no case to bring against me.

D.I. Cartland came himself to see me later that week to say that they had found no evidence to link me to any of the murders and that they were satisfied that the witnesses who sparked off the investigation had been mistaken in identifying me as the person they had seen. He thanked me for my co-operation with the police and for taking the investigation with such good grace.

Chapter 41

During February, my long-time friend, Tom Rouse asked me out to dinner at the Imperial Hotel in Barnstaple.

This was not unusual as we often dined out locally.

After a very enjoyable meal, we retired to a lounge for coffee.

Tom said that he was worried about me. He had noticed some changes in my behaviour over the past two years and was concerned that I was in some kind of trouble. He had noticed that I was often away from home for a day or two and usually did not say where I was going. He realised that this was none of his business but said that in the past I had always been very open about where I was going. He had noticed through phoning me that I was always unable to take telephone calls while away, or that I was refusing to take his calls. The latter seemed unlikely so he assumed that I must leave the phone at home, which was not a normal thing to do.

He had read in the papers following the Barnstaple killings that some people around the country had reported to the police that I looked like a lady they had seen near the scene of one of the murders by the vigilante killer, on the day of the killing.

He knew that I held right wing views about the lack of justice and punishment for various criminal activities, and in particular, the crimes of Nigel Boland in Taunton. He had known my friend Sylvia and how I felt that Boland had been responsible for his death.

He said that he had been impressed with my quick and effective action in dealing with the terrorist killer in Barnstaple and how I had been cool and ruthless throughout this incident.

Tom next referred to my late husband's guns. He said that John had confided in him years ago that he had an automatic pistol and a long- range rifle which he had 'inherited' from his days in the army. He was aware that the spate of unresolved killings had all been carried out with similar ex-army weapons.

He then asked if I was the vigilante killer that the police were looking for.

I had remained silent throughout Tom's statement and question.

I responded: “No, I am not the vigilante killer although I tend to agree with some of the things that he or she has done. I feel somewhat flattered that you think that I am capable of carrying out such a series of complicated killings all over the country whilst leading a normal life of domesticity here in Devon at the same time”.

I told him that the police had been to see me in response to the reported sightings of me at the scenes of some crimes. They had searched my home, garden, and car for any evidence of my involvement in any crimes. They had taken away my personal computer and telephone to search them for any evidence and had found nothing to link me in any way to any of the crimes.

I told him that they had taken me to the police station and subjected me to several hours questioning about my lifestyle, places I had visited, and what my views were on how criminals should be punished and if I agreed with death sentences. At the end of all this the police had confirmed to me that they had found no evidence of any criminal involvement from the searches of my property or from the extended interview with me. They had explained that it was not unusual for people to mistakenly identify characters they saw on television, or whose photographs they had seen in newspapers as being connected with crimes.

I went on to say that I had not been aware that my behaviour pattern had changed over the past two years or that I had been away on more trips than usual.

I said that I regularly visit Taunton, Exeter and Bristol on shopping trips, and I sometimes stay away in hotels for a few days as a break from the normal routines.

I explained that I really liked the relationship that he and I had, which was uncomplicated and irregular which is why I had not asked him to accompany me on my trips away.

As far as the guns my husband used to have John had at my request arranged to dispose of these at an early stage in his illness. He took them away one day and I have no idea where they went. If Tom knew where John kept the guns, he was welcome to see if they were still there or not.

I told Tom that I was not offended by his suggestion that I might be the vigilante killer as there was circumstantial evidence that it could have been me, and as already explained the police had been thinking along the same lines as him.

Tom said that he believed me but that to fully put his mind at rest he would like to examine the place where John kept the guns which he understood was in a recess under a loose floorboard in a bedroom.

I said that I was very happy for him to do this and led him upstairs to my bedroom. I pushed back the bed to expose the loose floorboard and pointed it out to Tom. He knelt down and lifted the floorboard to expose the empty recess. He felt all around it with his hand and then replaced the floorboard. He apologised for doubting me and assured me again that he believed it was not me. He hoped that his doubting and suspecting me would not damage our friendship.

After Tom dropped me home and then drove away to go to his home, I mulled over what had been said.

I fully understood how Tom felt. My behaviour had changed, and his suspicions were of course correct. My close association with Tom was actually placing me in danger of being detected.

Chapter 42 - April 2024

When his father was murdered in Taunton, Martin Boland told the police that the security camera covering the front door entrance did not have a recording facility and that there was no footage of the killer at the door. What he did not tell them was that he monitored and recorded activity on that camera on his telephone, as part of his task of ensuring the security and safety of his father.

His recording showed an elderly woman carrying a bag, arrive at the door and ring the doorbell. When his father answered the door, she produced a pistol from the bag and without speaking shot him dead.

Martin did not know what her motive had been for killing his father and had no idea on who she was. Her face was clearly visible on the recording, and he determined that he would track her down and kill her in revenge for his father's death.

He followed the police investigation as closely as he could and as weeks and months went by it became clear that they had no idea who the killer was and had not even established that it was a woman.

He studied every elderly woman he saw but was unable to find her.

Following his father's death, he took over his role as leader of the drugs business with the same team of people. He let it be known that he believed that the police's conclusion that his father's murder was a gangland killing by one of his rivals simply meant that the police had no clues as to the killer's identity. He also let it be known that he was determined to establish who the murderer was and to get revenge on the killer and any accomplices once his identity was established.

On 12th January 2024, sixteen months after his father's death he was watching the national news on TV when Lorna Cooper gave a live interview following her heroics in stopping and killing a terrorist gunman in Barnstaple. He recognised her immediately as his father's killer. He got his mother to watch the News at 10 with him that evening and she also agreed and confirmed that Lorna Cooper was her husband's killer.

They agreed that they would wait until the media interest in Lorna Cooper subsided and would then visit North Devon to check out her routines and decide how best to kill her. They would do this job themselves without involving any of their crew and hopefully no-one would ever know of their involvement.

On Wednesday 3rd April, Martin Boland drove to North Devon and visited Rishlew, the village where Lorna Cooper lived and found her house. Her car was on the drive, so he guessed that she was in. He studied her property layout and all her neighbour's properties with a view to arriving and leaving discretely at a later date. He drove out of the village and parked in a lay-by between the Village and Barnstaple. He was delighted when, two hours later, Cooper's car passed him on its way to Barnstaple and was driven by the target woman. He drove back to the village, parked on the square and walked down the road towards Cooper's house. He walked down her drive and rang the doorbell. There was no response. He looked around and could see that there was no camera in the porch. He walked around the house checking doors and windows and searched for any security devices. He found none. The garage was open, so he had a look inside this. There was also a log shed with an unlocked door and inside were logs and some garden tools. Feeling satisfied that he understood the layout, he walked back to his car and drove the 50 miles home.

He would carry out further reconnaissance visits over the next few weeks to establish the pattern of Lorna Cooper's lifestyle.

He would dress differently each time and use a different car each time to reduce the possibility of being noticed.

Chapter 43 - April 2024

When I returned home from shopping on Wednesday 3rd April, I saw that my camera recording device had become active. A year earlier, I had installed a good quality secret camera on the roof of the bungalow, which was triggered by movement, It was installed inside the gable eave of the roof, with just the lens exposed, and, from the ground, it was impossible to identify it as a camera. It recorded a short video of anyone or any vehicle which came down my drive heading for the front door. It also recorded any person or vehicle leaving the drive. The recording could then be accessed either on a PC or telephone.

The recording that day was of a well-dressed man in his early twenties. It was ten minutes before he returned to leave the drive, which made me very suspicious. What had he been doing on my property for ten minutes! I checked all around the house for signs of a break-in, but nothing appeared to have been tampered with.

There was something familiar about him and I felt sure that I had met him somewhere. As he had behaved suspiciously, I assumed that he was connected in some way with one of my killings.

The following day, I visited Exeter Library and researched the newspaper coverage in the local and national papers following each of the killings. After an hour of searching, I found a photograph of the Boland family at the inquest of Nigel Boland the previous year. Nigel's son Martin Boland was the man who had visited my property the previous day.

Clearly Martin Boland had somehow identified me as his father's killer or had seen in the papers that I had been questioned by the police about the murders. His behaviour alerted me to the possibility that he was planning to avenge his father's murder. His actions yesterday had all the signs of a reconnaissance trip similar to many I had conducted myself.

The first thing to do was to recover the pistol and some ammunition from its storage area. I would then plan how to prepare for the possible visit of a hitman. The following day, I recovered the pistol and took it home.

If the police searched the bungalow again, they would find it, but this seemed unlikely.

It was probable that the visit would be under cover of darkness and would aim to catch me unprepared. Assuming it would be a gunman, he would either break-in to the bungalow or try to lure me to open the front door. I decided that for the next few weeks, I would sleep in the log shed. My mobile phone would alert me if the security camera was triggered should an intruder visit. Although an intruder could gain access to my garden without using the entrance drive, I felt that any intruder would want to be able to make a quick getaway and would therefore have a vehicle and would use the drive as an entrance.

The log shed already had an electric light and an electric socket. Using the wheelbarrow, I moved all of the logs and stacked them against a wall in the garage. Then I swept the floor of the shed and put down a piece of carpet I had in storage. I purchased a fold-down bed and mattress which just fitted in the shed. Next was to put in a small convector heater, which made no noise and generated warm air. Finally, I put an armchair in the shed. There was a small window at the side from which I could see the front door. I oiled the lock and the hinges to ensure that the door could be opened silently.

That evening, I retired to bed at my usual time of 11pm by leaving and locking the house and locking myself into the log shed. I plugged in my phone to charge and set it to ping if the roof camera was activated by an intruder. I did not undress but just took off my shoes and covered myself with a duvet. The loaded pistol was on the floor beside the bed. I surprised myself by sleeping soundly until 6.45am when I got up and went back to the house for breakfast. I locked the shed door, and hung a cloth over the window, so that nobody could see my new quarters.

For the next few weeks, I lived cautiously, keeping the gun close at all times and monitoring all movements on the external camera. The car was parked where anyone approaching it would be seen on camera. The only external trips I made were to town once a week for shopping. I stayed in the house and did no gardening. Every night, I slept in the shed from 11pm to 7am in darkness and in silence.

In the early morning of Sunday 28th April, my phone vibrated quietly at 1.10am. I got up quietly, put on my shoes, and picked up and cocked the pistol ready for firing. Standing well back from the window, I was able to see the front door. There was a man at the door wearing dark clothes and a Police Officer's Peaked Cap. The security light above the porch had come on and I could see that the man was Boland. He had a pistol in his hand, which he kept down by his side and towards his back. He rang the doorbell three times, which I heard clearly, and waited. After a minute, he repeated the ringing and waiting. Whilst I was pleased that I had correctly anticipated this visit and had prepared accordingly, I felt scared and sick to the pit of my stomach at the danger I was in and what I must do to save myself.

I unlocked the shed door silently and opened the door a few inches without a sound. I was about 10 metres from the man. He was facing the front door of the house with his back to me. Ideally, I would have liked to move closer to him but could not risk him hearing me approach so instead I held the gun with my arm outstretched and took careful aim. I shot him in the head hitting him to the left of his ear. He fell forwards into the porch and remained motionless.

In case he had an accomplice keeping guard on the road at the drive entrance, I remained in the shed standing inside it with it the door ajar.

Almost immediately, a woman came running down the drive calling "Martin are you all right"? She screamed when she saw him lying in the porch and ran to him.

I had little option but to deal with her also. I stepped out and approached her with the gun aimed at her head. When I was just two metres away, I shot her in the head. Both were dead. The woman was in her sixties, so I assumed that she was a trusted driver, or a relative, perhaps his mother.

A factor which had worked hugely in my favour was the fact that I am an old woman. Boland could not let himself consider that an old woman could be a sharp-witted opponent against him. He actually had thought that all he had to do was to knock at my door, wait until I opened it and then shoot me. That was of course what had happened to his father. He would not have made the same mistake if I was a young man.

Whilst no longer in personal physical danger I now had a serious problem on my hands. These two bodies had to be removed, and they were each heavier than me.

I waited in the shed for a few minutes in case there was a second accomplice, or a neighbour had been awakened and came to investigate. Whilst waiting in the shed I gave some thought to the situation. I would have to find a way to remove and hide the bodies and to move their car which was probably parked at the entrance to my drive. All was quiet.

I checked that both people were dead and then walked up the drive to the road. As anticipated a car was parked at the entrance. There was a quiet hum from the car, and I realised that the engine was running. It was an electric car. I got into the car and drove it down my drive and parked close to the front door.

The woman was lying across the man and there was blood all over the porch. I could not lift the woman, so I went and got the wheelbarrow. By lying it on its side beside the woman I was able to heave her body into the wheelbarrow and then somehow, I managed to pull it up onto its wheels with the body sprawled inside it. I opened the boot of the car and by pushing the wheelbarrow to the car and putting the front of it against the back of the car I was able to lever it upwards until the body fell forwards into the boot. I pulled back the wheelbarrow and pushed the legs into the boot and closed it.

Getting the man's body into the car would not be so easy.

He had to go onto the rear seats of the car. The central armrest could be pushed up into a recess which turned the rear seat into a bench seat. After racking my brains, I got my ironing board from the utility room and placed it as a ramp from the ground to the rear seat of the car. I then got a rope from the garage and tied it around the man's body under his arms with the knot at the back. By putting the rope across the rear seat and out the opposite door and then tying the rope to a rear hitch on my car I was able to tow the body, inch by inch, up the ramp and into the electric car. This was hard work and time consuming as I had first to position both cars to enable the heaving operation to work and had to go to reposition the body a few times to get it into the car. When done, I untied the rope from the body and from my car and went and got a picnic rug from the house to cover the body.

There followed a major clean-up. There was blood everywhere. I ran the garden hose with a high-pressure nozzle and washed the side and rear of the Boland car, the rear of my car, the ironing board, the rope, Boland's gun, the front door the porch and the drive. The ironing board was impossible to clean so it would have to be disposed of, so I put it in the car over the body on the back seat. I dried Boland's pistol and put it in the glove compartment of his car as there was no reason to keep it.

I was covered in blood from all the lifting and pulling so I went inside and had a shower. All of my bloody clothing went into the washing machine which I then set to run and put it going. I cleaned the inside of my car as the front seat and steering wheel had become bloodied. Then I decided to quickly tidy the log shed.

I took the duvet and the telephone and charger over to the house and locked the shed. I had not yet decided where to drive the electric car to, but clearly, I would have to make my way home without a car. I was annoyed with myself for not planning all of this earlier. I had spent weeks sleeping in the shed and knew that if Boland came to get me, he would have a car.

I put on waterproof walking shoes, and warm clothing and put a waterproof overcoat in the car. I hid my pistol in the recess under the floorboards in the bedroom. Finally, I put £500 in notes into my trouser pockets.

I made a bowl of cornflakes and a cup of tea as it might be some time before I would eat again. I put on vinyl gloves which I would keep on until the car was abandoned.

I drove the electric car out of my drive shortly after 3am and headed for Exmoor, which was in the direction of Taunton where they had come from. I would leave the car somewhere close to Taunton. Once I was a mile from home, I stopped the car to study the controls as I had never driven an electric car before. I established that there was up to 150 miles of power remaining which was ample for my requirements. I learnt how the lights worked including dimming and indicating. The actual controls for driving were similar to petrol driven cars with accelerator, brake and automatic gear changing. Satisfied that I knew the essentials, I drove on trying desperately to work out where best to leave the car.

I decided, as I drove, that the car with the bodies needed to be left somewhere near Taunton where Boland lived. In that way, when found it would look like a gangland killing, although forensics would later establish that the bullets came from the vigilante's gun.

During the drive across Exmoor, I stopped at the entrance to a wooded area and carried the ironing board about two hundred metres into the wood and dumped it in a ditch. I hated having to do this as I detest fly-tipping, and here I was indulging in such unacceptable behaviour myself.

I knew of a woodland area just a few miles outside Taunton in the Blackdown Hills area, south-east of the town. I needed to avoid driving through Taunton as the car might be recognised so I stopped and put Thurber Woods into the Sat-Nav. The resultant map would take me through the outskirts of the town which was not acceptable. I chose a different route bypassing Taunton altogether through Wiviliscombe and by-passing Wellington. This added about 10 miles to the journey but would be much safer. On the journey from home to Thurlbear Woods, which was sixty-two miles, I met only seven cars coming towards me and none passed me. Devon and Somerset are so peaceful in the early hours of the morning.

Thurlbear Woods are managed by Somerset Wildlife Trust. When I arrived there, I stopped and opened the main entrance gate which was unlocked. Closing the gate behind me I drove deep into the woods and onto one of the walking path routes until I saw a suitable place to leave the pathway altogether and drive into the woods. I drove a few hundred metres before the terrain became too thickly vegetated with shrubs, grass and dead tree branches for the car to go any further.

Much as I dreaded seeing and touching the two bodies again, I had to do it as I had remembered that their telephones had to be retrieved from the scene and disposed of later. I easily found Boland's mobile in his trouser pocket but was unable to find a mobile on the woman's body in the boot. I felt sure that she would have had one so proceeded to search the car for it. Thankfully it was in the glove compartment under the pistol. Although I could get rid of the phones, I was not sure if the police would be able to track where the phones had been on that fateful evening.

During the phone search I realised that the rug covering him was mine and would need to be removed from the scene in case it could be traced to me. Before leaving the car I carefully went through a checklist in my head to ensure that I was leaving no trace of myself behind. When I had first driven the car from the road to my front door, I had not been wearing gloves, so I cleaned the steering wheel and the door handles and panels with a handkerchief. Thereafter I had worn vinyl gloves during all my time in the car. I considered covering the car with foliage to hide it but decided that this would be too time consuming and difficult.

It was quite dark in the woods, but I was able to retrace the route the car took from the pathway into the trees. At the pathway, the car had flattened the grass and foliage as it entered the woods. Using a leafy branch, I brushed the area as best I could to remove the signs of entrance. I guessed that by 9am, when walkers started passing the spot, the grass would have risen again, and nobody would suspect that a car had gone in there.

The walk back to the entrance of the woods took ten minutes and I then set off walking to Taunton at 5.20am. It took me an hour and a half to walk to the railway station. When close to the town centre I put the picnic rug in a skip in a supermarket carpark. I had already put Boland's Police Hat in a wastepaper bin. I removed the SIM cards from both of the confiscated mobiles and snapped them in half. These, I later flushed down a toilet in the railway station. As I crossed a bridge over the river Tone I dropped the two phones into the river.

Normally I am very much against polluting the land or rivers with rubbish, but ‘when needs must the devil drives’.

As I neared the station, a police car pulled in beside me and an officer asked if I was alright. I replied that I was fine and was on my way to the station to catch an early train to Bristol. This explanation seemed to satisfy the two officers, and they drove on. This exchange with the police had made me panic a bit, but then I realised that they were simply curious to see an old woman walking on her own so early in the morning. Anyway, there was nothing I could do about it. Hopefully they would forget about me after a few hours. Age was on my side here. If I had been a young attractive woman they would have remembered me for months.

The first train to Bristol Temple Meads was departing at 8.27am. I purchased a return ticket to Bristol and settled down in the empty waiting room. What a night! For the first time since 1am I let my body relax and I suddenly felt very tired. I had a first-class ticket which was reasonably priced on Sundays and fell asleep as soon as the train left the station. This train took the coastal route to Bristol and stopped at numerous stations. I slept through them all and was awakened by the guard when the train arrived in Bristol at 9.31. I tore up the return ticket to Taunton and flushed the pieces down a toilet. Felt much better.

I had breakfast in the station and caught a train to Exeter StDavids at

10.55. I could not risk sleeping on this train in case I slept all the way to Plymouth. Arrived at Exeter station at 11.52 and caught the next train to Barnstaple at 1.20pm. Slept again and woke in Barnstaple. The taxi home took twenty minutes. Had a snack and went to bed in my own bed indoors.

On Monday morning I removed the furniture and carpet from the shed and replaced the logs and garden tools as before.

Then I phoned both of my children to have chats with them. After that I spent a few hours in the garden planting crops which should have been planted weeks ago.

I decided to keep the pistol, armed and ready, close to me at all times at home. At night, it would be kept by my bedside. If members of Boland's gang knew of their plan to murder me, they might decide to finish the job on their behalf. On balance, it was probably unlikely that they had shared their plan as it would have been far safer for them to employ a hitman to kill me rather than put themselves at risk. I reasoned that this was a job that Boland wanted to carry out personally. But in case I was wrong I would remain on high alert for a few months.

I was worried about the fact that the mobile telephones of Boland and his female accomplice had been to my home and back to Taunton during the night. Although the telephones had now been disposed of, I did not know if the technology of mobile telephone providers could trace where a particular telephone had been on a given date. As there was nothing, I could do about this, I decided to forget it and not waste time worrying.

Every day I searched the Telegraph and listened to the BBC Radio Somerset news bulletins for news of the Boland's car having been found. It was three weeks before it was found, and it quickly became a big story. It was confirmed that the woman in the car was Jane Boland, Martin's mother and wife of Nigel Boland who had been my first victim. Again, the police initially felt that the murders were likely to be gang related.

I was reasonably confident that the police would find no evidence to lead them to suspect me. If they had been able to track where the Boland's phones had been on the night of the killing, they would have located their bodies much sooner. Forensics would link the bullets in the bodies to the same gun used for my earlier killings, but they did not know that the gun was mine.

Chapter 44

Despite being exonerated from each of the murders mentioned by the police I was aware that this was solely as a result of lack of evidence. I was left with a feeling that they would be keeping a close eye on me and that their investigations were not over. I decided to work on the basis that my telephone and laptop were both bugged so that my telephone calls would be monitored and everything I did on the computer would be seen and read by the police.

They had the run of my house and garden for a day whilst searching for evidence so there could be hidden cameras or microphones inside and outside the house and there could be a tracker hidden on the car. I would have to curtail my activities and take extra precautions to avoid giving them anything to work on. Over the next few weeks, I searched carefully for cameras, microphones or bugs in the house and garden but found nothing.

For the next few months, I led a harmless existence reading, gardening, having facetime calls with my family and getting involved in village affairs.

I continued to read The Telegraph daily, which kept me up to date with the news but there was seldom any mention of the various murders.

I still had the pistol in the house in case any of Boland's people came for me, but this was risky in case of another search by the police. At the end of June I decided that the pistol should be removed from the house and put with the rifle in its secret hiding place. On the same day I took the rifle home and cleaned and oiled both guns before wrapping them in an oily cloth and putting them away.

I was regularly invited to be interviewed on TV and Radio to relive the day of the gunman's attack in Barnstaple, but I managed to decline each of these. I was also invited to write articles for magazines and newspapers but again I politely declined these requests. I was surprised at the large fees' media organisations were willing to pay me for my services but luckily, I did not need extra money. I felt that it was better to stay out of the public eye rather than risk being identified by further witnesses.

It was difficult to establish how effective my killings had been in curtailing the activities of people involved in obstructive protests, drug dealing, shoplifting, and police abuse. I could only hope that I had made such people feel less secure and untouchable if they continued their illegal and anti-social activities.

Progress had been made in dealing with the 'Just Stop Oil' protesters. The police had at last been allowed to bring each protest to a speedy conclusion by arresting the protesters and charging them. Several protesters had been sent to prison and not surprisingly the number of disruptive protests had reduced dramatically.

They moved on to defacing famous works of art, in art galleries, by smearing them with paint. Whilst this was not disruptive to the public it was despicable behaviour and was viewed with disgust by most people.

Chapter 45

During January 2023 the police came to the conclusion that there was a serial killer carrying out vigilante murders. A murder in Taunton and a murder in Cheltenham had been established through forensics as having been carried out using the same gun. The murder in Southampton was carried out using a rifle but all three murders were of people who might be considered targets for a vigilante murderer with extreme right-wing views.

Scotland Yard appointed District Inspector Robert Cartland as the lead detective to track down this killer. He was an experienced detective who had helped to solve a number of murders over a twenty-five-year career, and he was pleased to have been given this task. With a team of three research assistants, he began by researching all unsolved murders in the UK over the previous five years to identify any similarities with the two recent murders. They found no evidence that there were links to any previous murders.

The first killing had been of a drugs baron, the second was of a major supporter of anti-social protestors. On the murder of Dudley in Southampton it was noted that the victim could be seen as anti-social and a risk to society through his behaviour and how he had almost killed a police officer.

D.I Cartland agreed that a strong link between these three killings was that all three victims could be seen as anti-social hate figures. Although the third victim had been shot with a rifle rather than a pistol, he felt that there was a strong similarity through the background of the three victims. It seemed likely that he was looking for a vigilante who was taking the law into his own hands and inflicting extreme punishment on his victims.

He still had no evidence to show if the killer was male or female, young or old, British or foreign, white or black.

The fourth murder to catch the attention of D I Cartland was of the hate preacher in Reading. Forensics confirmed that the bullet was fired from the same gun as was used on murders one and two. He was now convinced that the killer was a vigilante who was taking the law into his or her own hands.

The next murder on 26th July was of Turner in Ipswich. The first and most positive similarity was that the bullet came from the same revolver as used in murders one and two and four. The second was that the victim was an activist with the 'Just Stop Oil' movement.

When forensics established that the bullets that killed Boland in Taunton and Matthews in Cheltenham were from the same gun, the police knew that it was likely that the three crimes had been carried out by the same person.

To the extreme frustration of D.I Cartland there was again no eyewitness to this murder even though it took place in daylight in a public place. He still had no clue as to the identity of the serial killer.

He embarked on a major research project to see if he could identify if any car was in each of the murder locations on the dates of each murder. Taunton Council was able to provide him with CCTV recordings for 14th September 2022 of all vehicles entering or leaving Taunton on that day. This involved CCTV recordings from eleven different roads leading into Taunton including from Junction 25 of the M5 motorway. Taunton Council stored these recordings for three years. To go through all of this recorded data manually and list every car would have needed massive manpower if done manually. Instead, the police technical division devised a program using Artificial Intelligence to scan the numberplate of every vehicle and list and store every number.

Unfortunately, the Council in Cheltenham only retained their CCTV recordings for two months so were unable to supply any data to D.I Cartland.

The Southampton Council provided recordings for the main roads leading into the city including from the M27 but did not cover all roads. Ipswich had recordings covering 90% of the roads leading into city.

Reading Borough Council were able to supply footage from several city CCTV cameras covering the day and evening of Bukhari's murder.

Ipswich Council were able to supply CCTV footage from a number of locations near to the scene of the Turner murder.

Again, using an AI (artificial intelligence) software program, a police computer was able to search for matches for every car that entered or left Taunton on 14th September 2022 with all cars that entered or left Southampton on 27th December 2023, Reading on 27th March 2023, and Ipswich on 26th July 2023. This involved millions of searches but was completed in seven hours. There were twelve matches between Taunton, Southampton and Reading and four between Ipswich and Reading but none between Ipswich and Taunton or Southampton.

The owners of the sixteen cars were contacted and checked out thoroughly by the police but each could be definitely ruled out of any involvement with the murders.

A strange aspect of this vigilante killings case was that despite widespread media identification that there was a serial killer on the loose, there was no public outcry that the killer must be found and no public criticism of the police. Perhaps this was because there was substantial sympathy with, or support for, the killer. Alternatively, it could be because the general public did not feel threatened or endangered by the killer as the victims were apparently selected for anti-social activities or crimes.

In August, a killing took place in an Irish hospital of a prisoner who had been injured in a police shootout. It was reported that the killer was a woman but there had been no arrest.

A Fortnight after this killing, D.I. Cartland telephoned one of his counterparts in the Irish Garda Siochana to explore the possibility of a connection with the UK killings. He was assured that the Irish killing was carried out by a rival gang to the victim and that the police had a good idea who the perpetrator was and were gathering evidence against her. Following this conversation, D.I Cartland was satisfied that there was no connection between the Irish killing and the UK killings.

Following his visit to Barnstaple to interview Lorna Cooper he remained very suspicious about her. It would be an extraordinary coincidence if Lorna Cooper turned out to be the vigilante and had then become actively involved in the Barnstaple terror incident. His impression of Cooper whilst interviewing her was of a gentle person, of limited intellect, who would not be capable of planning, carrying out murders, and leaving no real clues for the police. However, this perception might be incorrect, and she could be a good actress and a skilled operator.

He asked the Barnstaple police if they would keep an eye on her as best they could but ruled out tapping her phone or placing cameras or microphones on her property. He did however get authority to put a tracker on her car so that they would know where she went. The Barnstaple police were requested to put the tracker device on her car and to monitor her car's movements. The device would need to be small and well-hidden either within the car or on the outside as he

felt that if she was the person they were looking for she would search the car thoroughly for any tracker or listening devices. The Barnstaple police agreed that an unmarked car would check her house daily in case she removed the tracker. Barnstaple police would monitor the cars movements and would immediately inform D.I, Cartland whenever she drove away from North Devon.

Although Cartland was determined to identify and apprehend the vigilante he had a certain amount of sympathy with the killer. As a long-serving police officer he was fully aware that the British legal system was soft on crime. The police were continually frustrated by the sometimes impossibly high levels of evidence required before the Crime Prosecution Service would agree to prosecutions. He was also aware that the judicial system itself was too lenient with sentencing and that slick lawyers could often get criminals off on technicalities. He knew many criminals who had managed to avoid prison for years and were able to continue their illegal activities unhindered.

As an avid reader of history he knew that crime could be brought under control by being tough on crime and having real deterrence.

Back in the 15th Century King Henry V imposed law and order throughout England by ruthlessly putting down rebellions by lords and dukes. There were many examples in history of tough rulers imposing strict law and order.

Singapore was a good current example of a state that has reduced crime to a minimum by being tough on crime.

His search for the vigilante would continue. He knew that if the culprit was not apprehended there was a serious danger that there could be copycat crimes by another person having seen that the first vigilante was not apprehended and affectively had escaped punishment.

Chapter 46 - September 2024

He spoke with an Irish accent and said that his name was Michael Doody and that he was from the Garda Siochana in Ireland. He was the police officer who had been guarding Adrian Reilly in an Irish hospital. He assured me that he was not here to see me on official business but that it was purely a social call. He showed me his Warrant Card and ID. I offered him tea, which he declined.

He explained that he was on holiday in Devon with his wife A man visited my house one day during September and I recognised him immediately. He was the Irish police officer who had been guarding the prisoner in the hospital in Drogheda in August the previous year. I suddenly felt very afraid as it meant that, at last, I had been tracked down, I was working in the garden when he arrived, and I invited him into the house. He said that he would be perfectly happy to have a chat with me outdoors, so we sat at my garden table. I was pleased that we would talk in the garden as I was still suspicious that the house was bugged by the police. I had searched the garden table and seats several times and was satisfied that there were no hidden microphones.

but had made a point of seeing me as he had something to tell me. I felt very nervous. He said that he had been on duty in The Lourdes Hospital in Drogheda during August last year guarding a patient who was ill.

I asked him where Drogheda was, and he just smiled.

He continued by saying that the patient he was guarding was a gangland boss who had been captured and was awaiting trial. His conviction was by no means certain, and the trial was likely to go on for a long time and would cost the Irish Government millions of Euros. On 10th August, an intruder entered the patient's room and shot him. He had then come face to face with the armed intruder in the hospital corridor and had been held at gunpoint. The intruder was a woman. He had felt sure at that moment that he was about to be shot dead, but instead the woman had risked leaving him alive as a witness to her crime and had left using the hospital stairway, putting herself at further risk of being caught. He was grateful to this woman for two reasons.

The first was for killing Adrian Reilly. He was a notorious gangland criminal who dealt in drugs and was responsible directly and indirectly for the deaths of several people in Ireland and in the UK. He had also destroyed the lives of hundreds by getting them addicted to the drugs he supplied. The Gardai had been trying to get evidence against him for years and having at last arrested him, were not confident of a long sentence conviction. By killing him, the woman had rid Ireland of a brutal gangster and killer. It had been embarrassing for him personally that he had failed to prevent the killing of Reilly whilst guarding him, but he had been able to cope with the criticisms that came afterwards.

The second reason he was grateful to the woman was for sparing his life and increasing the risk of getting caught herself. Normally a hitman would immediately kill any witnesses to a killing, and this was what he expected when the woman confronted him in the corridor.

He said that when he saw me being interviewed on TV on the day of the Barnstaple multiple killings, he knew by recognising my face and my voice that I was the woman who assassinated Reilly the previous year. The wig and glasses had altered my face somewhat, but he was still able to see immediately that I was the killer.

On the day after my statement on TV, he had a phone-call from one of the Garda officers who had stopped and searched me, and my car close to the border with Northern Ireland a few hours after Reilly's assassination. He had arranged a meeting with the officer and her colleague later that day. The female Garda said that she had recognised from the TV that Lorna Cooper was the woman they had searched a few hours after Reilly was shot. Her colleague who had searched the car said that he had also recognised her. When they stopped her near the border, she had silver grey hair in a bob and was not wearing glasses. They could make a positive identification. They were both aware that Garda Doody was very grateful to the assassin for not killing him and that he was glad that Reilly had been killed. They too were glad he had been killed and understood why Garda Doody was grateful to have been spared. The Gardai had never released to the press that the female assassin had an English accent and as a result of this the criminal fraternity of drug dealers in Ireland were convinced that the assassin was a member of one of the drug gangs and had put a lot of time and effort into trying to identify this female killer.

They had then agreed between the three of them not to report my discovery to their superiors or to the British Police. If I did get caught for any of my crimes, it would not be down to them. He then congratulated me for my brave and decisive actions when confronted with the gunman in the salon in Barnstaple.

I started to reply but he stopped me and said, “Lorna, please do not reply to all I have just said. I don’t want a confession or a denial. My purpose today was to put your mind at rest about being identified by us, and to thank you for sparing my life. Having reviewed the UK killings that you were possibly involved in I can see that in each case the victim was a person who probably needed to be punished but was unlikely to be punished by the police or the courts. Whilst as a police officer, I cannot condone your activities, I privately applaud you for some of them. I strongly advise you to stop your vigilante activities immediately, before you inevitably get caught. I will now leave you and wish you good luck for the future."

He stood up, gave me a hug and a kiss on the cheek and turned and left the garden.

I decided there and then that it was time to retire.

THE END

.

ABOUT THE AUTHER

Brian Sherwin wrote this debut novel, Autumn Career, at the age of 79. Born and educated in Ireland he moved to Devon in England in 1972 where he has had a long and successful career in business. Married to Eva, Brian has four sons who each live and work in the South-West of England. His motivation for this book was that few novels have leading characters in their seventies and older people are capable of great and terrible deeds.

Autumn Career

Printed in Great Britain
by Amazon

54323135R00233